INFERNO

RACHEL GRANT

BOOKS BY RACHEL GRANT

Flashpoint Series
Tinderbox (#1)
Catalyst (#2)
Firestorm (#3)
Inferno (#4)

Flashpoint Series Collection

Evidence Series
Concrete Evidence (#1)
Body of Evidence (#2)
Withholding Evidence (#3)
Incriminating Evidence (#4)
Covert Evidence (#5)
Cold Evidence (#6)
Poison Evidence (#7)
Silent Evidence (#8)
Winter Hawk (#9)

Romantic Mystery
Grave Danger

Paranormal Romance
Midnight Sun

This one is for Gwen Hernandez.

From that first night of pulling an all-nighter together as we both did mad revisions on a deadline, to years of answering all my odd questions about military life and the endless beta reads you've given me, you are so much more than a critique and plotting partner. Thank you for being a dear friend.

Djibouti City, Djibouti
June

A harsh boom split the air, followed by a series of sharp, loud, rumbling bangs, startling all six people in the US embassy conference room. The burst of explosive sound went on too long to be a sonic boom and caused the windows to rattle and light fixtures to swing. For it to shake the building like that, the explosion must've happened nearby.

Alarm coursing through her, Kaylea Halpert jumped to her feet and ran to the window. A cloud of smoke billowed a few blocks to the northwest.

"Is that the UAE consulate building?" Margaret Shaw, the embassy management officer, asked.

"I think it's closer," Chris Crawford, the deputy chief of mission, said.

"It *is* closer," Kaylea said. She knew every landmark between the US embassy and the

United Arab Emirates consulate. "Car bomb?" she speculated.

Chris hit the intercom button on the phone next to his seat at the head of the table. With the ambassador on leave due to a family medical emergency, Chris was in charge. "Stephanie, implement emergency protocols until we have more information. Full embassy lockdown, and get Camp Citron's base commander on the phone."

"Yes, sir."

It took several minutes, but finally, Captain O'Leary was on speakerphone. "I just got off the phone with the head of the local gendarmes. A car blew up a few blocks from the UAE consulate. There's some damage to nearby buildings and cars. As of right now, reports of injuries are minor, but it's too soon to know. Special Operations Command is scrambling a team to cordon off the area for local authorities. We believe they will invite the FBI to aid the investigation as it relates to terrorism."

It was too soon to know if the explosion had anything to do with the US, and given that the bomb had gone off closer to the UAE consulate than the US embassy, there was a chance this might not involve them at all. But with Djibouti being home to the US military's only permanent base on the continent as well as being the front line for fighting al-Qaeda on the Arabian Peninsula—known as AQAP in intelligence circles—even if it wasn't directed at Americans or American assets, the explosion would definitely be the US's problem.

And as she was a case officer for the CIA, Kaylea's assets might be able to provide key intel.

"Thank you, Captain," Chris said. "We are implementing high-threat-level security protocols."

"I will send a team of marines to provide additional security for the embassy."

"Thank you," Chris said and ended the call.

He met Kaylea's gaze. "You want to accompany the FBI to the scene?" Chris was one of the few who knew exactly who and what she was. There was no place for secrecy in embassy hierarchy.

"Yes." She had an asset inside the UAE consulate, and others could be drawn to the scene as well. As the American embassy's community liaison officer and being fluent in French and Arabic, she had a role in working with local officials to ensure the US provided the support they needed to deal with this attack. And maybe she could speak with her assets and get some HUMINT—human intelligence—that would shine a light on what had just gone down in the streets of Djibouti City.

He nodded. "Before you go, we have one item left on our agenda that involves you."

She cocked her head in question. This had to be important if it needed to be addressed now. Tensions were high as Eritrea and Ethiopia moved closer to peace and factions wanted to stop that. The situation in Yemen was getting worse, and the US's role as reluctant ally to Saudi Arabia in Yemen's ongoing civil war was becoming untenable. The bomb blast could be about any of those situations, which everyone in this room was tasked with handling with diplomacy.

As if secret prisons, torture, and civilian-killing airstrikes in Yemen could be erased with polite relations.

"Tomorrow night, I'll be attending a black-tie party hosted by Saudi businessman Sheikh Rashid bin Abdul al-Farooq. Al-Farooq has been doing his best to position himself as a great philanthropist and benefactor for Dji-bouti, and the ambassador requested I go in his place. Just this morning, I received a request that you, Kaylea, attend as well."

Her stomach dropped the moment he'd said the name al-Farooq. She'd met the man a month ago during one of the press events an-nouncing the Linus fossil find, and he'd taken undue interest in her.

Al-Farooq, who'd adopted the honorific "sheikh" due to his supposed status in the busi-ness community—and not because he was head of family or a leader in the Muslim community —was new on the scene as a power player in Djibouti, and both the CIA operator and diplomat in her wanted to know why. Usually the opportunity to spend time with a man like al-Farooq would be right up her alley, but thanks to intel Freya had passed on to her just yesterday, she believed this particular Saudi businessman was in deep with Russian Bratva, and she had zero chance of turning him. The consequences would be dire if he betrayed his Russian backers.

"I don't want to attend a party at the Saudi embassy. The protocol is too rigid for me as a woman to be able to do my job." This was true for both of her jobs—as community liaison and case officer.

"The party isn't at the embassy. Al-Farooq had a lavish estate built on the Gulf of Tadjoura that was recently completed. This is a house-warming of sorts. Representatives from every embassy and consulate in Djibouti will be there, along with the biggest players in business from each nation. As community liaison, there's good reason for you to go." This too was true for both of her jobs.

Events like this were the perfect opportunity to identify potential assets or put pressure on people she was trying to recruit. But al-Farooq's personal interest in her was worrisome.

Plus there was another problem. Just days ago, one of the highest-ranking supervisors in the CIA's Special Activities Division had been exposed as a traitor. And Kaylea had taken action that had helped expose the man.

Seth Olsen, they were just learning, had been owned by Russian Bratva—same as al-Farooq. It was also true that Olsen had been in Djibouti three weeks ago—and they weren't entirely sure whom he'd met with while here. He could have met with the Russians and revealed Kaylea's cover. Al-Farooq could know exactly who and what she was. He was, after all, con-

nected to the same oligarch—Radimir Gorev—
who was pulling Seth's strings in the end.

Her instincts said this party was too high-
risk at this moment in time. They needed to
know more about how much Seth Olsen had
betrayed the Agency before she could walk into
this kind of event to do her job.

As a covert operator, she wasn't risk averse,
but she also wasn't a fool. "Do you think
there's any chance the explosion would cancel
the party?" she asked the deputy chief, a little
too much hope in her voice.

Chris shook his head. "I wish, but no."

"I don't want to go." She sighed. "But he'll
take it as a slight." After all, the invitation had
been issued through diplomatic channels.

Chris studied her, concern in his eyes. But
then, she never balked at assignments like this.
Cozying up to men like Farooq was literally in
her job description. Well, for one of her jobs,
anyway.

"I could go as your date," the public diplomacy officer, Stephen Walker, offered.

She smiled at Stephen. He was a nice guy
and good at his job, but he wasn't the sort to
get someone like al-Farooq to back off. No. She
needed more muscle.

"Bringing a date isn't a bad idea," Chris
said.

"Yeah. That's why I offered," Stephen said.
"I'm full of good ideas."

She winced. Sometimes, even among diplomats, diplomacy was hard. "Thank you,
Stephen, but I need someone more intimidat-

ing. Al-Farooq turns violent when he's told no, and the fact that he's using diplomatic channels to get me to this party doesn't sit right."

"You could probably get one of the special forces guys from Camp Citron to take you," Stephen said, showing no sign he felt slighted that he wasn't badass enough to be her white knight for the evening.

She gave a slow nod. Freya could probably recommend one of the guys from Delta Force. They knew undercover work, and their commanding officer would approve leave from the base for the night.

But it hadn't been Delta operators who'd backed Freya when she was on the run in DR Congo with Sergeant First Class Cassius Callahan just days ago. Instead, Freya and Cal had been aided by Special Forces. Half of Cal's Green Beret A-Team had taken a risky, off-the-books mission without hesitation. And one of the reasons they'd done it was because Kaylea herself had raced to the base to convince Major Haverfeld and Captain Oswald that Freya Lange —known to them as Savannah James—wasn't a traitor.

Cal's A-Team knew all about Seth Olsen and his connection to Radimir Gorev. Those six men were among the only people who knew. All six would understand why she needed someone to watch her back. But the team had just gotten back from DR Congo yesterday, and they were supposed to head home soon. Odds were no one would have time to take a night off to play escort. Still, she could ask.

Of the six men who'd been in Congo with Freya, two didn't have girlfriends. Not that one of the attached guys couldn't play her date for the evening, but they'd be more convincing as a couple if the guy wasn't in love with someone else. She needed her date to be comfortable in the role.

Without hesitation, a face popped into her mind. Deep brown eyes capped by dark brows and a full head of thick, glossy dark hair. Warm brown skin evidence of his Puerto Rican heritage. And an even warmer smile.

The last time she'd seen him was just six days ago, when she'd rushed to Camp Citron to talk to Haverfeld and Oswald. When she first arrived, his eyes had swept over her with quick appreciation. Not objectifying, like a lot of the soldiers and sailors on base. More friendly. Respectful. But it was the hot spark that flared in his eyes when their gazes met as she left his CO's office that had stayed with her.

A spark like that...in the right conditions, it could start an inferno.

"I'll make some calls later," she said as she stood. She needed to get going if she wanted to accompany the FBI to the site of the explosion. She would ask Freya for Sergeant First Class Carlos Espinosa's phone number when she returned to the embassy.

S even more days. The words were a mantra as Carlos climbed into the back of the Humvee.

Seven more days and he'd be on a flight home. No more having his day scrambled by a car bomb. No more hundred-and-five-degree heat index. No more mess hall food.

Bastian—or rather, Chief Warrant Officer Ford when they were on duty—climbed into the front passenger seat. "Trainees are loaded and ready. Let's roll."

Ripley, their team's senior communications sergeant, put the beast of a vehicle in gear, and they were off, bouncing down the rutted track that passed for a road in Djibouti. Their Humvee was the first in a caravan of Humvees and buses. The ride was rough here, but in five miles, they'd be on the outskirts of the city and the roads would get slightly better.

Their A-Team had spent more than half the last year training Djiboutian soldiers to be guerilla fighters. With the explosion in the city, it was a perfect opportunity for the trainees to get real-world experience providing security in their capital. Within minutes of the blast, team and trainees had been gearing up for a mission that was not a drill. The trainees were hyped, blood pumping with excitement. The young men were ready for action.

For his part, Carlos was just glad to hear reported injuries were minor. No casualties. He didn't mind this field trip. Hell, it would make the hours pass faster, even if their workday would now stretch into the night.

He was so ready to leave the heat of Djibouti behind, anything that sped up the clock was fine with him. He could almost smell his father's cooking. Hear his nieces' and nephews' laughter as they splashed in the swimming pool.

There wasn't much chatter inside the Humvee. They were all tired after having spent the first half of the day working in the hot Djiboutian sun.

Carlos, along with five others from his team, had just returned from DR Congo yesterday, but today, they'd been back in the heat with the trainees as if they never left. There was simply too much to do before shipping out to rest for a day. Not that he or the others cared. They were all tired of being here. If working without a day off got them home one day sooner, they'd do it.

Callahan might be the only exception. Upon returning to Camp Citron, Cal had abandoned the Containerized Living Unit he shared with Pax in favor of Freya's private wet CLU. The team's senior weapons sergeant might not mind staying in Djibouti an extra few days, given that it meant more time with Freya.

Carlos had to admit he might not be so ready to return stateside if he had a beautiful CIA operator eager to share her bed with him. But then, he had a very specific covert operator in mind.

She had gorgeous brown eyes, flawless brown skin, corkscrew curls, and killer curves.

The woman was astonishingly beautiful in a way that reminded him of the musician and actress Janelle Monáe. She had presence and style. When she entered a room, eyes went to her as if pulled by a high-powered magnet. Her work for the American embassy meant she was always dressed as if she expected to run into royalty or diplomats. In Djibouti, seeing a woman in a designer business suit was rare. Add heels and a skirt, and it was rarer still. But given the way she *looked* in her formfitting skirts and knee-high boots...men took one look at Kaylea Halpert, and their brains scattered.

Or maybe it was just Carlos's brains, but he didn't think so.

The reaction had to serve her well as a CIA case officer, which was probably why she dressed as she did in a place where her style was far from the norm. Of course, she'd never admit to working for the CIA, but he'd been certain for months, starting the day he'd seen her at the base firing range practicing with a variety of weapons. She'd been a crack shot with everything she touched.

Community liaison. Right.

The woman was brains, beauty, and badass.

His favorite combination.

And when this deployment was up in seven days, he'd probably never see her again.

They reached the city block where the bomb had gone off. The explosion occurred a quarter kilometer east-southeast from the UAE consulate, and the US embassy was just a half klick away to the south-southeast.

Most likely someone was trying to get the attention of the UAE, but nothing could be taken as a given.

The busload of trainees unloaded, and Carlos rounded up the group he'd been training in building and demolition. As a combat engineer, Carlos knew how to build a bridge, and he knew how to destroy it. He would lead his select team of trainees in inspecting the nearby buildings for damage.

The others on his A-Team directed their trainees to fan out and cordon off the block.

It was a smooth operation, the Djiboutian soldiers fulfilling their duties as if they'd done it a hundred times. They had, actually, but only in training.

Their polished execution today was enough to make Carlos's homesick heart proud. He led his team to a group of gendarmes and got the lowdown on the investigation and inspections so far, then they headed for ground zero.

As they approached, his view of the crater was blocked by ambulances and fire trucks. Carlos nodded to Goldberg and Washington— the A-Team medics who were standing by with their trainees—as he passed the row of ambulances.

Upon first glimpse of the crater, he'd guess they'd used C-4, which raised a lot of questions. A few months ago, C-4 had been planted under Dr. Morgan Adler's rental car. The archaeologist hadn't known about the explosive on a timer as she drove straight for Camp Citron, only to be stopped—and saved from dying in the blast—by Pax and Cal.

Everyone thought Etefu Desta had been behind the bomb under Morgan's car. But Desta was in US custody—captured by Pax, Cal, and Bastian after the warlord had Morgan abducted— and after her rescue, Morgan said Desta had claimed a minister had been behind the bombing.

That minister was still in power, and now here was another car bomb on a timer, with the possibility of C-4 as the explosive. Perhaps the message here wasn't meant for UAE after all.

Carlos spotted a man who must be FBI speaking to a gendarme and a firefighter. He headed in that direction and almost stopped short when he recognized the woman to the fed's right.

His brain wanted to do its usual thing when he saw her and blank out. But this was work, and a lifetime of intense training took over, thank God. He gave Kaylea a polite nod and introduced himself to the fed and explained that the trainees were there to inspect the buildings closest to the blast site.

The man smiled. "Your XO told me you were on the way. Thank you. We could use your help." He nodded to the soldiers. "I mean their help."

Carlos nodded. It was satisfying to be able to turn over the security of the country to its own countrymen, and he was proud of the role he'd played in that process.

The fed then gave Carlos a full rundown of

what they knew so far—including that he suspected the explosive agent had been C-4.

Carlos met Kaylea's gaze at that. Being CIA and tight with Freya, she had to know everything about Morgan's car bomb. Had she connected those dots too? How much did the feds know?

One of them should interview Desta, wherever the warlord was being held.

Carlos turned to the half-dozen trainees under his command and translated the fed's words into Arabic, giving them instructions on the buildings they would clear.

Kaylea then addressed the men in Arabic as well, saying she was concerned about the building adjacent to the one closest to the blast site. It held offices she'd visited several times in her work, and it wasn't structurally sound.

He would wonder which of her jobs she referred to, but she wouldn't have said a word if it was the covert one. That she was supremely competent in both her jobs impressed the hell out of him.

Brains, beauty, and badass.

He turned and had taken two steps toward the building when Kaylea spoke softly, stopping him in his tracks. "Sergeant Espinosa, when you're done inside the buildings, could you spare a moment? I have a request."

He allowed his eyes to skim down her body for the first time since arriving. Like everyone else in the blast perimeter, she wore a Kevlar helmet and vest, but that was as far as the safety gear went. Sturdy jeans or an Army

Combat Uniform weren't Kaylea's style. No, she wore one of her narrow skirts that hugged her round ass, and his favorite kickass knee-high boots.

Only Kaylea could look like a fashion model in this place and time.

Hell, she made Kevlar look hot. And not in the sweltering, miserable-to-wear-in-the-desert kind of way.

"This is gonna take some time," he said. "Could be hours."

She nodded. "That's fine. I'll be here. If you can find me when you're done, I'd appreciate it."

"Sure thing."

Her gaze flicked over his shoulder, and she took a step toward him and placed a hand on his chest. Or rather, his Kevlar. *Damn Kevlar, always in the way.* She smiled and if it weren't for his years of training, he might've been blinded by the radiance. "Be careful in there, Sergeant."

He gave her a quizzical look but smiled back. "Always, Ms. Halpert." With their unusual exchange complete and his promise made, he led his team into the building.

2

Kaylea turned back to the FBI agent before al-Farooq could make a play to catch her eye. He was beyond the perimeter guarded by the Djiboutian soldiers. She hoped to hell they'd keep him out, but if he caught her eye and she ignored him, it would be taken as a slight.

It was odd seeing the wealthy businessman standing in a crowd like any commoner. But then, diplomats and VIPs were pouring in in droves, gawking at what could have been a tragedy, held at bay by the line of soldiers Espinosa's team had delivered to the blast site.

One would think the VIPs would be afraid of more explosions, but that didn't appear to be a concern.

She returned her gaze to the crater in the roadway. What was the point of this explosion?

She'd caught Espinosa's look when the FBI agent had said "C-4." She'd bet he was wondering if this was connected to Morgan Adler's car bomb. It didn't surprise her that Espinosa was as quick to make that connection as she was. He was smart, he knew Morgan, and he was an explosives expert. He knew how rare C-4 was here—at least among the groups who would be the most likely suspects for this type of bombing.

If Boko Haram or al-Shabaab could get stockpiles of C-4, they were all in deep trouble.

She spent the next hour taking photos, consulting with the FBI agent, on the phone with headquarters, and talking to the local officials.

It was damn hot wearing the Kevlar vest and helmet. How did everyone in the military do this all the time? On the Horn of Africa, eleven degrees north of the equator, no less. If she'd ever questioned her decision to go for covert work instead of military, this answered it.

The crowd beyond the perimeter grew, then shrank as the heat sweltered with nothing to see. Al-Farooq must've left, because she caught no further glimpses of him and breathed a sigh of relief, which proved to be premature because ten minutes later, when she was on the phone with Chris updating him on the scene, al-Farooq got past security and made a beeline for her.

Dammit.

If they were in Saudi Arabia, it would be inappropriate for him to greet her in public. In this instance, she'd welcome that custom.

She quickly got off the phone and gave the man a bright smile. "Sheikh Rashid bin Abdul al-Farooq, *as-salaam'alaykum.*"

"Miss Kaylea, *wa 'alaykum salaam.*"

"I'd say it's a pleasure to see you but…" She spread her hand to encompass the devastation of the explosion.

"And I am surprised to see you in such a dangerous place, Miss Kaylea."

She didn't mind his using her first name only nearly as much as she minded being called "Miss" and not "Ms." Her job at the embassy was all about respecting the protocols and customs of others, but some men refused to grant her the same courtesy and use the title she preferred, no matter how many times they were told.

"The Djiboutian soldiers are doing a fine job seeing to everyone's safety, and I've been able to be of help here with my language skills," she replied.

"I have been eagerly awaiting word from your embassy about the invitation extended to you," al-Farooq said.

"I am honored by the invitation but alas have been here and unable to respond."

"Will you be my guest tomorrow evening?"

"It is my pleasure to accept. Now, I must beg your pardon, Sheikh, I am needed—" She cut off her words when she spotted Espinosa making a beeline for her.

Thank you, Lord.

"Carlos!" she said, running toward him, then launching herself at her unwitting savior. She was breaking ten different kinds of protocol in leaving the sheikh without proper farewells, but she'd claim to be overwrought with emotion. "I was so worried," she added as she landed against his body armor and wrapped her arms around his neck.

His arms circled her waist, and she caught the surprise on his face as her mouth met his. She kissed him as if it was a thing she'd done before. Maybe even often.

And oh, when his mouth met hers, she knew it was something she wanted to do again. And often.

This public kiss was an even worse offense than abandoning the sheikh without following proper protocol. But dammit, the man creeped her out, and this was the perfect way to establish she wasn't available.

Plus, Espinosa had big muscles and a big M4 carbine rifle slung across his back, which was readily visible to the Bratva-owned Saudi businessman. The State Department would just have to cut her some slack.

Espinosa kissed her back, his closed lips lingering on hers, soft and tender, proving tongues didn't have to touch for a kiss to be intimate. She wished she could lose herself in the moment, but instead, she leaned back to see the smile playing about his mouth and a warm light in his eyes. "Well hello, Kaylea," he whispered.

She played with the hair at the back of his neck, beneath his Kevlar helmet, and smiled back. "Sorry," she whispered. "If you get in trouble for the PDA while in uniform, I'll explain to your XO." A public display of affection while in uniform was yet another taboo she'd just broken.

"It was worth it." His eyes crinkled at the

corners. A lifetime in the sun and, she presumed, a lot of smiling had given him early laugh lines. He was a beautiful man. "I take it that was for the benefit of that guy in the keffiyeh who's staring daggers at me?"

"Yeah. I can explain when he's gone. I need to go back and finish our conversation."

"Want me to go with you?"

"Better not. But watch my back, please, until he leaves."

"You got it, sweetheart."

When other men called her sweetheart, she was usually irritated. But it wasn't a condescending nickname coming from him. He'd said it like he meant it. Of course, she *had* just very publicly kissed the guy.

Heat shot through her as he leaned down and brushed his lips over hers in a soft, fleeting kiss. Behind him, a soldier—Washington, maybe?—let out a catcall.

He released her, and she turned back to al-Farooq, who was indeed staring daggers.

Too bad. So sad. I am not your plaything and never will be.

She squared her shoulders and set off to face the angry businessman.

🖋

Carlos's day had just taken a strange but appealing turn. Damn. The closed-lip kiss hadn't lasted long and it had only been for show, but somehow, it still had been intimate.

And it had felt so damn natural, as if she'd greeted him that way dozens of times.

He watched as Kaylea quickly dispensed with the guy they'd put on the show for. Carlos would feel guilty for shifting his focus from the explosion, but he had no doubt whatever was going on with Kaylea was also related to national security and the US mission in Djibouti. He was still serving his country. Just maybe a bit more eagerly when her mouth was involved.

She waited until the man was beyond the security line before turning and approaching Carlos. As she neared him, she nodded to a nearby building entryway, and he followed her to the alcove where they could speak in private.

Inside the arched doorway, she pulled a tiny device from her pocket and flicked it on. White noise emitted from the small speaker. Louder than he would have expected for such a small device. "It's both a signal blocker and white noise, so we can speak relatively freely," she said.

"What's up, Kaylea?" Until a few minutes ago, he'd never called her by her first name, but she'd called him Carlos before planting one on him, so he figured it was okay.

She smiled. "First, thank you. That man is a Saudi businessman who has a propensity for violence when he doesn't get what he wants, and I have reason to believe he wants me. I don't know if his desire stems from actual lust or if Seth Olsen blew my cover, but either way, I want nothing to do with him."

He was shocked by her frank admission. "You're admitting you work for the CIA?"

She nodded. "You already guessed when you saw me at Camp Citron last week, plus I have a huge favor to ask, and it relates to my cover."

"You need me to kiss you again?" He couldn't help but tease. "Because I have no objections."

She smiled. "Actually, maybe. I mean, more kissing could be required."

"I'm in. For my country, I am willing to serve."

She snickered. "You are a fine patriot, Sergeant Espinosa."

The light of warmth in her eye and her laughter gave her already stunning face a special glow. He needed to keep his focus. Joking aside, he was on duty, and so was she. "What do you need?"

"Tomorrow night, that businessman— Sheikh Rashid bin Abdul al-Farooq—is hosting a black-tie party at his brand-new palace. He wants me there, and given State Department protocols and our current relationship with Saudi Arabia, it would be unwise for me to refuse. But given the current situation within the CIA, it would also be unwise for me to show up without a big, strong, handsome Special Forces soldier as my date." She smiled up at him and batted her eyelashes. "Carlos Espinosa, will you do me the honor of taking me to the ball?"

He was neatly trapped. Given the public kiss in front of the sheikh in question, she could hardly show up with someone else as her date. He couldn't say no if he wanted to. Good thing he didn't want to. "I'll need signed orders to leave the base. If my CO agrees, I'm yours."

"I'll have Chris Crawford—he's running things while the ambassador is in the US—call Major Haverfeld." She frowned. "But will this be a problem? I know you're scheduled to return home soon."

"Not for seven days. My team can spare me for one night. But once I'm gone, you'll be on your own with the sheikh again."

"I'll deal with that problem later. Maybe I can find another special forces boyfriend."

Suddenly, Carlos wasn't quite so eager to go home.

She turned off the white noise, and they left the alcove together, walking back toward where his team was gathered, giving Captain Durant a breakdown of how the trainees had performed. He needed to provide his own report to their A-Team captain.

As they neared the others, Kaylea said, "You're going to need a tux or dress uniform. Frankly, I'd prefer the uniform. It presents more authority."

He frowned. Dress uniforms weren't the sort of thing one packed for deployment. An idea sparked, and he called out, "Chief Ford, where did you get the blue mess you wore in Morocco?"

"Frey—uh, Savannah James ordered it."

"Any chance she ordered enlisted blue mess too?"

He made a face. "I'm pretty sure she did. She wasn't sure I'd play along when she ordered it, so I know she got a few different sizes. Probably different ranks too."

He looked at Kaylea. "I'll check with her when I get back to base. She might have something I can use."

"If not, I can get you a tux from the embassy."

"It's a date, then. What time should I pick you up?"

"I don't actually know. I'll email you when I get back to the office."

"Better yet, text me." He pulled out his phone. "What's your number?"

She gave it to him, and he sent her a text so she'd have his, just like this was a bar pickup back home and not the site of a car bomb in Djibouti City.

Plans settled as much as they could be, she rose on her toes and kissed his cheek. "Thank you, Carlos. See you tomorrow." Then she walked away, her perfect round ass swinging as she traversed the bombed street in those sexy, kickass black boots.

Next to him, Sergeant Dion Washington let out a low whistle. "Dude, did you just get a date while on duty? In the middle of a blast investigation?"

"Yes. Yes, I did." Every guy there was watching the sway of Kaylea's ass, and he felt a ridiculous surge of male pride. It wasn't a real date, but these guys didn't need to know that.

"Jesus. Did you *see* how she kissed him?"

Sergeant Stockton said. "In the middle of the fucking street?"

"Kaylea Halpert. Kissed you. While you were on duty, wearing your ACU." Dion shook his head as if he'd just seen a unicorn prancing down the closed street.

"Worth the reprimand that's coming your way?" Bastian asked.

They all knew there was zero chance there'd be consequences for a kiss she'd initiated, but his answer was the same either way. "Hell yeah."

"I can't wait to tell Janelle," Dion added. Janelle was Dion's deployment fling. Except they all figured he planned to ask the Navy medic to marry him before they shipped out on Saturday, so she wasn't a fling after all.

"Kaylea Halpert." Goldberg said her name with deserved reverence. He clapped Carlos on the back. "My man, you have just achieved legendary status."

3

The date started like any other. Well, except for the fact that Carlos had to sign out a vehicle from the motor pool using authorization forms signed by his XO, and then he left the base by presenting another authorization form at the serpentine gate.

So maybe not like any other date at all.

But once he was freed of the military installation, he was on the open road, on his way to pick up a beautiful woman to escort her to a fancy party. Officially, he was on leave until oh seven hundred tomorrow, but he expected to be back on base much earlier. Kaylea had said she hoped they could just put in a token appearance and leave.

He wore a dress uniform he'd managed to get from Freya. It was a strange feeling to be driving by himself across the desert in dress uniform. But then, it was weird to be driving at all, regardless of the type of uniform. In all his months in Djibouti, he'd never left the base alone. And to leave the base for a night out was unheard of. When he wanted entertainment, his evenings had been spent in Barely North, the club on the base. The rest of his evenings had been spent in the CLU he shared with Ripley, reading or on his computer.

But here he was, alone in a vehicle for the first time in over six months, crossing the desert to pick up his date, who happened to be a brainy, beautiful, badass spy.

He really was living his best life.

Kaylea lived in an apartment not far from the embassy. She met him at the door, and he let out a low whistle as he took in her appearance. Her makeup was as flawless as her warm brown skin. An intricate sideways braid ran above her forehead and around, disappearing into a large puff ponytail that made a crown out of her wild corkscrew curls. The style highlighted her perfect features. The line of her nose, the delicate slant of her eyes, the point of her chin, and the long, slender column of her neck.

Her dress was a silky, airy thing in a mosaic of blues and greens that covered her shoulders and arms to below the elbows, and landed far below her knee. He assumed the modest lines of the dress were for their Saudi host. The gown avoided being too tight or revealing, while somehow draping her curves in a way that was still incredibly sexy.

Brainy, beautiful, and badass.

Damn. He wished this date were the real deal.

She smiled as her gaze moved down his

body. "I do love a man in uniform. Remind me to thank Freya for being thorough in her mission planning." She stepped back, and he entered her home.

The furnishings were simple and elegant, much as he'd expected from the woman who exuded class and style even when visiting a bombed street. "We have a half hour before we need to head out. Would you like a glass of wine?"

He needed to remain alert tonight, but one glass wouldn't hurt. They settled on her couch, each with a glass of a very good pinot noir. The warmth that spread through him had nothing to do with the alcohol content and everything to do with the flow of energy in the room.

From Kaylea's body language, there was nothing fake about this date.

"Will you tell me your real name?" He hadn't realized how much he wanted to know until the words slipped out. But then, he liked hearing her call him Carlos—when deployed, everyone called him Espinosa or Espi—and he wanted to give her the same gift, even if it was forbidden.

One corner of her mouth kicked up. "Actually, Kaylea is my real name."

"No way."

"Yes. Given my background, my real identity is the best cover there is."

"How long have you been a case officer?"

She shook her head. "I really can't talk about my work. I'm sorry."

"It was worth a shot."

She took his glass from his hand and set it on the side table next to hers. "You know what else is worth a shot?" Her smile was sweet and just a bit wicked as she hiked up the skirt of her dress and straddled him. She settled on his lap, and his cock sprang to life to greet her. She let out a soft sound deep in the back of her throat, and said in a breathy voice, "This." And then she kissed him.

Unlike the kiss in the street yesterday, this was openmouthed. Hot. And deep.

Her tongue stroked his in as carnal a kiss as he'd ever received. And the woman of his fantasies had initiated it without hesitation. His hands circled her waist and slid up her back, holding her close as their mouths explored and tasted.

Kaylea the badass spy was in his arms. Holy hell, this was better than anything he'd imagined.

She raised her head and slid back, still on his lap but no longer pressing against his ready erection. "Wow." Her voice was soft and so very hot. She stroked his cheek. "I wanted to do that once without an audience."

"You can do it more than once," he said.

She laughed. "I'd curse the party we have to go to, except without it, we wouldn't be here right now." She continued stroking his freshly shaved cheek in a way that made him think she liked his smooth skin. "And I like this."

He could get lost in her deep brown eyes. "I've wanted to kiss you since that day at the firing range. It was so damn hot watching you shoot. But then, I like watching everything you do."

"You made me so nervous at the range. I wanted to impress you."

He placed a hand behind her neck and pulled her head down until her lips were just above his. "I was *very* impressed." Their mouths met in another hot kiss.

Damn. This wasn't what he'd expected when he drove through the serpentine gate earlier this evening. He hadn't dared to hope for this.

Maybe he could ask Major Haverfeld if he could stay on for another few months. He didn't need to go home anytime soon.

She raised her head again, ending a second spectacular kiss. "Party," she said, more than a bit breathless.

Crap. The party. This wasn't the time to get lost in foreplay when they had a formal event to attend.

She rocked her hips, pressing herself to his erection. Her eyes closed, and she let out a soft mewing sound. "You're free until seven a.m., right?"

"Yesss." Damn, she felt good. Felt right.

She brushed her lips over his in a soft kiss. "Thank you for agreeing to be my date, Carlos."

His open palms ran over her backside. "I'll always have your back, Kaylea."

&

Al-Farooq's new Djiboutian home truly was a palace. Before leaving her apartment, Kaylea showed Carlos aerial photos so he'd know what to expect. The home had been constructed several miles outside the city on a spit of land overlooking the Gulf of Tadjoura. The property was circled by a stone wall. Inside the wall was a long circular drive with a fountain in the middle. The house itself was centered on the land and was capped by three round domes, a small one marking the entryway, a large one behind it, and the third on the other side of a massive courtyard with circular gardens and what was sure to be a lavish pool, assuming it had been finished. The aerial photos had been taken before construction was completed.

Given the scarcity of water in Djibouti, the lush green of the completed portion of the landscaping was appalling enough. Children begged for water on the streets here. Not food. *Water.*

"What a prick," Carlos said. "That fountain and pool had better be filled with ocean and not fresh water."

In the car, she gave him details about al-Farooq that she couldn't share over the phone or in text messages. Nothing in writing. No communication of substance that could be intercepted was the rule. Before they set out, she scanned the SUV Carlos had checked out from the base for listening devices.

"Al-Farooq is a relatively new player. I haven't quite sorted out his family history or his rapid rise, but he's got money which I'm fairly certain came from Russian Bratva and not Saudi oil, which is one reason I'm so uneasy about him."

"Freya's former boss, Seth Olsen, was also owned by Bratva."

"Exactly. I asked Freya if al-Farooq was at Russian oligarch Radimir Gorev's kompromat party in Tanzania, and she said she didn't see him, but he was on the guest list. We know that Seth Olsen was concerned about Freya's research into Drugov and Gorev—and both oligarchs were in deep with Russian organized crime. My personal concern is when Olsen was here in Djibouti, he met with his Bratva handlers. We suspect he revealed Freya's identity to the Bratva who were trying to recover Drugov's assets. He might have compromised my cover along the way.

"If so, al-Farooq could know what I am, and that could be his motive for inviting me to the party." She studied the handsome soldier at the wheel of the vehicle. "Thank you for coming with me tonight. I feel better knowing I'm not entering the house alone."

He glanced to the side and briefly met her gaze. "I'm glad you asked me." His voice was serious. No jokes about kisses and patriotic duty.

He was in soldier mode now, and she liked how he took the job seriously. She'd liked the teasing and kissing too, but this man was the soldier she needed when she needed him.

"I'll follow your lead on protocol for meeting and mingling, but one rule we need to

set now is we stick together once we're inside.
If they say you need to go off with the women,
we're leaving."

"Agreed. I don't think that will be an issue.
The party isn't at the Saudi embassy, and I was
specifically invited in my capacity as a US embassy officer, so I shouldn't be expected to
spend the evening with only women when
other embassy officers will be socializing with
the politicians and embassy officials from other
countries."

"You really are a diplomat, aren't you? You
do the work of a community liaison officer. You
have the credentials?"

"I am and I do. The 'embassy employee' title
that many case officers bear can wear thin with
overuse. The fact that I'm actively seen performing my work as community liaison sup-
ports my cover, and it gives me access to the
people I need to meet to obtain assets."

"Cal and I both figured you were CIA after
the day we saw you at the firing range. Plus
there was the time you were with Freya at
Barely North."

"Yeah. She and I decided meeting at Barely
North was unwise considering most of SOCOM
knew she was CIA and it was better not to have
people looking at me too closely."

"Sweetheart, men can't help but look at you
closely."

Again, she liked the endearment from him.
And the compliment. She'd looked at him
rather closely herself. There had been a few
times in the months since his team arrived that

her work as community liaison had intersected with his work training Djiboutians, and he'd caught her eye more than once, but it was that day at the firing range when she'd really noticed him. At the range, they'd talked and laughed and had not quite flirted.

She couldn't identify what it was about him that had caught her interest. It was just…all of him. He was funny, but knew how to be serious when appropriate. He'd showed her respect— none of that, "let's teach the little lady how to shoot" bullshit. And he was seriously hot. Just the way he'd said, *"Well hello, Kaylea,"* after she'd kissed him yesterday had been…perfect. Sweet, sexy, surprised, amused, a bit cocky, and loaded with masculine energy.

"My goal is to have people look at me and see a competent bureaucrat with a taste for fashion. Basically, as someone to underestimate outside of diplomatic channels."

"So the fact that you always look like you're on your way to a fashion shoot is part of your disguise?"

She smiled at that. "To a certain degree. I also really like a well-tailored skirt-and-jacket combination. And I have an expensive shoe fetish."

"The boots you always wear are damn hot. It's too bad they don't go with that dress."

She glanced down at the stilettos on her feet. She adored these heels, but like Carlos, she wished she were wearing the boots, although for a very different reason.

"If I hadn't seen you at the firing range and

then later with Freya, I doubt I would have guessed you were a case officer. You're good at your embassy job. Did the CIA teach you diplomatic liaisoning, or was that a skill you picked up elsewhere?"

She laughed. "I have a master of arts in international relations and diplomacy and I'm fluent in Arabic, French, and a few other languages." Arabic and French were Djibouti's two official languages.

"So, I'm going to go out on a limb and guess you're qualified."

She laughed again. "A little bit, yes."

"Brainy, beautiful, and badass."

Warmth flooded her. "You do have a way with words, Sergeant Espinosa."

He took her hand in his and brought it to his lips, keeping his eyes on the rutted road. "I like it when you call me Carlos."

The brush of his lips on her hand triggered a reaction far greater than a simple gesture like that should. "Carlos," she whispered.

The smile that tugged at the corners of his mouth was nearly irresistible. She wanted the party to be over with so they could explore this heat that kept flaring between them.

"So how did you end up in the CIA?" he asked.

"My parents are both professors—Mom is a linguist and Dad is an historian. I was an undergrad on 9/11 and had planned to study French in college—following in Mom's footsteps. But Dad's influence and constant reminders that we need to know our history

tugged at me too. Post 9/11, I wanted to understand what had happened and what would
come next, so I went into Middle Eastern
studies and began taking classes in Arabic. I
met a man in my Middle Eastern studies classes
and we fell in love. His dream was to be in the
CIA. Mine had shifted to diplomacy. But then
we invaded Iraq, which had nothing to do with
9/11, and I was confused by the CIA's role in
that. Simon—my ex-husband—and I spent
hours debating what the CIA got wrong and
why. We married when we were both in grad
school, and through it all, his dream of joining
the CIA after he had his masters never
wavered."

The college years with Simon had been
great. She'd been so in love, so certain they
would go the distance.

"I was skeptical about the CIA, but he convinced me to apply once we both had enough
postcollege work experience. Initially, I wanted
to be an analyst, but I applied for the Directorate of Operations because it was what Simon
wanted. He'd applied before me and was hired
before me. He worked for several months at
Langley before starting his stint at The Farm.
While he was away, I began my training at Langley—I was in the training class that followed
his.

"Just weeks before he would have completed
training, he quit. It's a weed-out program, and
he broke. It changed nothing about my feelings
for him. I loved him and supported him, but he
had trouble dealing. He was shocked when I

continued on with the CIA. He expected me to quit because it was his dream, not mine. He got a job at the State Department around the time I left for my turn at The Farm. I thought his new job would make it easier for him—he had a fantastic career ahead of him. But when I made it through training at The Farm, his ego suffered another blow. It became pretty clear he'd been rooting for me to fail, and that was…hard to take."

Hard. What a simple word to encompass so much pain. She remembered the hurt when Simon had insinuated they'd gone easier on her because she was a woman and the raging fight that had followed.

"Six months after I completed my training, we split. Simon is a good man. Part of me will always love him. But he couldn't deal with the fact that I'd succeeded where he failed, that I was living his dream, and that I refused to quit to ease his ego. I didn't quit because somewhere in the process, it had become my dream. I love both my jobs. And I'm damn good at them."

"Do you keep in touch with your ex?" Carlos asked.

She nodded. "He's at the State Department in DC, so our work lives still intersect. He remarried about nine months ago."

"I thought your divorce was recent?"

"Technically, it was—we didn't file the paperwork until he wanted to get married again. It was easier to let people believe the breakup was recent too. It's gentler to turn someone down by claiming to be still nursing a broken heart."

"Are you still nursing a broken heart?"

"No. He emailed me last month to tell me his wife is pregnant with their first child. I'm happy for him—truly and completely. He's finally made peace with his career, and he's found love again. He couldn't do that with me as a reminder."

"Do you want to find love again? Marry? Have kids?"

"I don't know. Right now, my second job is much easier as a single woman. Either job could require me to move at a moment's notice, and that can be hard on a spouse. Plus, being a covert operator is dangerous, and I don't like the idea of putting anyone I love at risk."

She'd put the notion of love and relationships behind her when her marriage dissolved and she accepted her first overseas assignment. Now she'd been working dual jobs for over four years, and Djibouti was her second overseas assignment. She had neither time—nor prospects—for relationships. This night with Carlos was the closest thing she'd had to a real date since she arrived in Djibouti. It hadn't even occurred to her that it *could* be a real date until she'd impulsively kissed him on her couch.

Now she wished she'd asked him out months ago.

"What about you, Carlos? What led you to join the Army? Why Special Forces?"

"When I was sixteen, my family moved from Puerto Rico to St. Petersburg, Florida and opened a restaurant. They weren't new to the restaurant business. My dad is an excellent chef, and they'd had a small restaurant in San Juan. They sold it to finance the one in Florida. The restaurant did well for several years. I was a junior in college—studying structural engineering—when the recession hit and the business began to fail. I dropped out of school to help out behind the line and in the front of house, but it was too late.

"My folks were too far in the red before they told me they were struggling. The restaurant closed less than six months after I left school. I considered going back to school, but the scholarships I'd had were gone and they'd only covered about half my tuition anyway. My parents couldn't help me, and I'd have to take on more debt. Basically, the Army looked like my best prospect because after I did my stint, I could use the GI Bill to finish college. But once I was in, I set my sights on Special Forces. I wanted to be a combat engineer. And here I am."

"Do you still plan to use the GI Bill to finish college someday?"

He shrugged. "Maybe. But right now, this is what I want to do."

She liked his easy answer. He was content in the path he'd taken, even if it hadn't been a straight line, or even what he'd planned at the start. She hoped that Simon had found the same contentment. Once upon a time, it had hurt that Simon couldn't find it with her, but now she only wished him happiness. After all, he was the one who'd set her on her own twisting path.

"And your parents? What are they doing now?"

He smiled. "A few years ago, they opened a new restaurant. Smaller. Like the one they had in San Juan. My sisters and I helped them get it off the ground. It's doing well. I've been counting the days until I can visit. There's nothing like going home to Dad's cooking."

"You said you worked behind the line—did your dad teach you to cook?"

He nodded. "I can hold my own in the kitchen."

He might just be the perfect man. Content with his path in life *and* he could cook? Next he would tell her he loved giving two-hour-long back rubs. "How old are you, Carlos?"

"Thirty-one. You?"

"Thirty-four."

"You like working abroad?"

She shrugged. "For the most part. I do get homesick, though."

He nodded, and she guessed he understood, given his job also sent him all over the world for significant periods of time.

"So who all is going to be at this party?" he asked. "I take it lots of VIPs and diplomats."

"There'll probably be about two hundred guests, but only a few dozen people who have a stake in the current political landscape."

"I don't suppose there'll be name tags."

"Oh, that would be heavenly. But no. You

won't be expected to remember names, though."

"Just let me know who you want to steer clear of." He paused. "If you...need to talk to an asset alone, I'm sorry, but that wouldn't be a good idea. I need to stay by your side."

"I wouldn't try to talk to anyone tonight. Too many opportunities to screw up and get made. And given the fact that my real name is what I'm operating under, if I'm exposed, I'm done. So don't worry. If I run into an asset, we'll speak in code to set up a meeting."

"Oh. Like 'the bird flies at midnight into the mouth of the lion' kind of code?"

"No. More like, 'I take my tea with sugar' versus 'I take my tea with cream.'"

"You better hope your asset remembers what that means. They ever reverse it?"

"Too often. But usually when that happens, they've done it on purpose. They're getting paid to be informants, and the longer they draw it out, the more money they get. Not a lot of incentive to speed things along. So they misinterpret a code to keep things going. It's a game."

They reached the arched entryway to al-Farooq's estate. As they drove under the ornate, arched gates, she said in a quiet voice, "Abandon all hope, ye who enter here."

4

Kaylea's words proved apt. This place was hell. Carlos stared around the room, filled with rich and/or important people to the political landscape of the Horn of Africa. The men wore tuxes, and the women—who made up less than twenty percent of the guests— wore gowns or abayas. Many wore full-face veils, and their hair was covered. But there were women dressed similar to Kaylea as well. Modest dresses that remained stylish.

But Kaylea was by far the most beautiful woman in the room, and Carlos could tell he wasn't alone in that opinion as male gazes followed her everywhere.

If this were America, he'd stand close and probably place a hand at the small of her back, but this was a Saudi man's house in Djibouti, and he needed to be respectful of the customs of both host and host country. Instead, he stood close by her side, not touching her, while still making it clear they were together.

Kaylea introduced him to a sea of diplomats

and politicians who, with the exception of the president and a few key ministers of Djibouti, he remembered by nationality only. One of the ministers was the man Morgan had suspected of planting C-4 under her car.

They left the ornate entryway—a domed room large enough to be a ballroom all by itself, and which he not very fondly dubbed "limbo"— and as expected, the next circles, or rather rooms, felt somehow worse. As if this place was built on a foundation of greed and suffering.

It didn't help that Kaylea had shared stories of al-Farooq's Bratva ties and he'd been forced to shake hands with the Djiboutian minister who might've planted a bomb that could have killed not just Morgan, Pax, and Cal, but also, if she'd made it all the way to the gate, could have taken out several marines on security duty.

A corridor separated the front domed room and the massive domed room that was the actual ballroom. Before they entered the main room, he glanced left and right down the corridor, which was long and extended the width of the house. Farther down, he saw doors on one side and archways that probably led to corridors that spanned the width of the massive palace.

In the aerial view, the pool and gardens had been enclosed within the structure—a lavish, centered courtyard. He'd expected the party to be held there, but it looked like the majority of the guests were gathered inside, under the largest dome.

Kaylea smiled and slipped her arm through Carlos's and said, "This way," as she steered

him into the ballroom and toward a small group
to the side of the room.

A white man in his midforties smiled at
seeing her. "Kaylea, you look stunning as
usual."

Her smile widened. "Thank you, Chris." She
turned to Carlos. "Sergeant Carlos Espinosa, I'd
like you to meet Deputy Chief of Mission Chris
Crawford."

Carlos extended his hand and received a
firm shake from the man who was second-in-
command at the embassy. "Thank you for
agreeing to accompany our Kaylea tonight,"
Crawford said.

"I'm honored to have been asked."

Kaylea spoke to the man on Crawford's left,
also white but probably a decade younger than
the deputy chief. "Stephen, I didn't know you'd
be here."

The man shrugged. "Yes. It's one of the reasons I offered to be your date. Another dull
evening. Might as well spend it with a pretty
woman."

Carlos kept his face carefully blank. It
wasn't as if Kaylea was an object to feel possessive over, and if this guy was interested in her—
enough that he'd asked to be her date—it was
really none of Carlos's business. But still, he
wanted to put his arm around her and stake a
claim he didn't have.

He liked her, pure and simple. And he
wanted her to be his.

"Well, now we're all here together," Kaylea

said like the diplomat she was. "Carlos, this is Stephen Walker, public diplomacy officer."

Another handshake and small talk, then Crawford said, "I'd better work the room a bit. My son has a stomach bug, and I'd like to get home to him."

"I'm sorry Joey is still sick," Kaylea said.

Carlos wondered what it was like to raise kids abroad like this. Since joining the Army, he'd lived on bases in the US and abroad, but outside the US, they weren't the kind of bases where family came along. Nothing like a career diplomatic post, in which families were part of the deal, even in unstable countries.

He studied Kaylea. Did she consider herself a career diplomat or a career spy?

This, of course, was not the place to ask that sort of question, but when they returned to her place, he was eager to know more about her work for the CIA. Odds were she wouldn't tell him anything, and he'd have to accept that.

His brainy, beautiful, badass babe had secrets.

"Al-Farooq is heading your way, Kaylea," Walker said.

The hand that gripped his arm tightened, but she gave no other outward sign of tension. She turned toward the approaching sheikh, her warm smile even reaching her eyes. Damn, but her control impressed him.

"Sheikh Rashid bin Abdul al-Farooq, *as-salaam'alaykum*," she said, giving the traditional Arab greeting, *peace be upon you*.

"Miss Kaylea, *wa 'alaykum salaam*," he

replied, giving the traditional response, *and unto you, peace.*

The man's gaze raked over Carlos and his uniform, the irritation that crossed his face making it clear he recognized Carlos from yesterday. "And who is this you have brought me?" he asked in English.

"Sergeant First Class Carlos Espinosa, please meet Sheikh Rashid bin Abdul al-Farooq."

The sheikh took Carlos's hand in a firm grip. He debated greeting the man in his own language, but instead opted for thickening his Spanish accent. "It is an honor to meet you, Mr. Farooq. Your home is quite magnificent. Like nothing I have ever seen." He glanced upward at the ornate dome that capped the circular room. He'd spoken the truth; the artwork was exquisite.

The man nodded but addressed Kaylea in Arabic. "I am disappointed you brought a man with you. I had hoped to spend time with you this evening, to introduce you to my associates and give you a tour of my palace."

Carlos pretended not to understand. He studied Walker's face and tried to figure out if he understood al-Farooq's words. It was possible the American diplomat spoke only French and English.

Kaylea responded in Arabic. "You are too kind and gracious a host to wish to show me such attention during your celebration."

"We have much to discuss, Miss Kaylea. Please, come with me. Leave your soldier here to enjoy the food and drink and his American brethren."

"I'm afraid that would be unkind. Sergeant Espinosa speaks no Arabic or French. Surely he can join us on a tour of this magnificent palace?"

"He is military," al-Farooq said.

"And our countries are allies," Kaylea countered.

Al-Farooq gave a polite nod. "Alas, not everyone here is allied with the US, I'm afraid."

"I too am American," she said.

"Yes, and the men here would rather see a pretty face than meet a soldier who slaughters their children."

Carlos didn't have nearly as much practice feigning ignorance as Kaylea, but he kept his adoring gaze on Kaylea and held his body loose, hoping he showed no outward sign he'd understood every word. "Kaylea, my sweet," he said in heavily accented English. "What are you talking about?"

She turned to Carlos. "Sheikh al-Farooq is honored to welcome you as his guest and invites us to enjoy his food and drink."

She tugged his arm and pulled him in the direction of the center of the room, where a gigantic ice sculpture of an Arabian horse sat in the center of a lavish spread of food on a massive round table.

An ice sculpture. In Djibouti. Where it was brutally hot and water was scarce. The weeping sculpture kept the food chilled, he supposed, but it was all an homage to gluttony.

He knew events like this were extravagant by necessity, but given that across the Bab al-Mandab Strait—in English, the "Gate of Tears"—Yemen was on the brink of starvation, and outside the gates of this palace, children begged for water, it was a bit much.

This wasn't Saudi Arabia. This was Djibouti, a tiny country on the Horn of Africa that had no excess to spare. Everything about this party felt wrong.

A Russian man approached and spoke to al-Farooq in Russian. Kaylea was introduced, and she responded in Russian as well.

How many languages did she speak?

The exchange ended with the Russian leaving before an introduction to Carlos could be made. Al-Farooq addressed Kaylea in Arabic, "I must see to my guests. Please, enjoy the feast." He spread his arm to indicate the laden table and ice sculpture.

She gave al-Farooq a smooth smile and nod. "As you wish. *Ila-liqaa'*." *Until we meet again.*

Carlos wondered if the Russian had been oligarch Radimir Gorev. He thought he might have heard Gorev among the rapid Russian words, but didn't dare ask with so many around to overhear. The question could wait.

He plucked a date from a dish and popped it in his mouth, and Kaylea did the same. He had a mental image of feeding her the sweet, sticky fruit and wished they could bail on the party now. He reached for the dish of pomegranate seeds, but Kaylea stopped him. "Better not. You know what happened to Persephone when she ate those in the underworld."

He laughed. "Good call." He raised an eyebrow at the waiters circulating the room with trays of drinks. "I didn't expect alcohol to be served."

"Events like this can go either way, depending on the host's beliefs or who he's courting an alliance with. My guess is al-Farooq is more interested in an American and European alliance right now than he is concerned with courting Muslim countries."

"Yet he's establishing a home base"—he spread his arms to encompass the circular room with the high domed ceiling—"a palace, in Djibouti."

"This is where the military is—both the US and China. This is the place everyone wants to be, the next seat of power in Africa."

They spoke softly, but at the same time, he suspected what Kaylea said was known to everyone present. This was business mixed with diplomacy. Forget the US Congress, parties like this were now the room where things happened.

He leaned close and whispered in her ear, "Now that we've made our appearance and greeted our host, can we escape?"

She glanced around the room, a slow smile spreading across her features. "I don't see why not. Stephen is the diplomat more suited to this kind of event."

"Should we tell him we're leaving?"

She shook her head. "And give him an opportunity to ask us to stay? No. Better to ask forgiveness than permission."

"Let's go, then."

They worked their way back through the crowd, stopping and chatting with men Kaylea knew on their way to the exit. It took a full thirty minutes to make it out the door, and by the time they reached it, Carlos no longer even felt guilty they were bailing so soon. They'd spent a solid hour at the party, and in that time, he'd heard at least a dozen men refer to Kaylea as beautiful and nothing else.

Each time, the words had been directed sideways. Men spoke of her beauty in the same way Walker and Farooq had earlier. As if they weren't addressing her, but referring to an object. "Men would rather see a pretty face," and "Might as well spend an evening with a pretty woman."

She was a face and nothing more.

But she was so very much more.

Once they were back inside his vehicle, after she scanned it for bugs, he said, "Hearing the way men talk about how beautiful you are makes me ashamed of the way I've done the same thing. You are so much more than a beautiful face."

She placed a hand on his knee and squeezed. "You don't say it like they do. I like it coming from you." She turned in her seat and leaned toward him. Her lips brushed his ear, and it was all he could do to keep the vehicle on the rutted road. "But then, I really like you, Carlos. Brains, brawn, and badass. Plus you're damn hot."

He smiled at that. He liked this woman. A lot.

She leaned against his arm, and they rode in silence for the long drive back to her place. When they were just a few blocks away, she said, "We didn't really eat at the party. We can stop at a restaurant, or have dinner at my place. I've got pasta, I think."

He considered his uniform. He was a little overdressed for a restaurant in Djibouti City. "Pasta is fine with me." He glanced sideways at her. He didn't want to make assumptions. "I can also head back to base if you want to say good night now."

"No!" The word was sharp and quick. So very different from the woman who'd controlled her every facial expression inside al-Farooq's palace. "I mean...no, please, I'd like you to stay for a bit if you can. If you want to."

He parked in the nearest open street parking space, a half a block from her building, and turned to face her. "I want to, Kaylea. Very much."

He wanted to kiss her here and now, but they just had a short walk to her apartment, where they would have complete privacy and he could kiss her in a way that would be so very inappropriate on the street.

They didn't touch or hold hands on the way to her apartment, but their steps were hurried. Just shy of breaking into a jog. And her in stilettos.

At last, she was fumbling with the key and got the door unlocked. Inside, he closed the door behind him and turned to reach for her. She held up a hand and pressed a finger to her lips, then pulled out her bug scanner and methodically cleared each room.

He waited by the door, not making a noise as she disappeared into what he assumed was her bedroom. Two minutes later, she returned. The bug detector was nowhere to be seen and she no longer wore the airy gown.

Now she was barefoot and wearing an orange silk robe.

His heart pounded and his dick throbbed. How the hell had he gotten this lucky? From the smile on her beautiful mouth, he knew he was about to get even luckier.

She stepped up before him, four inches shorter than she'd been a minute ago. She slid her hands up over the lapel of his jacket and pulled his head down, bringing his mouth to hers.

He slid his tongue between her lips, and she sucked on his offering. She made a soft mewing sound as he deepened the kiss.

His hands found her curvaceous ass, and he cupped it, pressing her into his body, his erection thick and hard against her belly. Her hands grabbed at his bow tie and yanked it off, then slid down and began removing the metal studs that held his shirt closed, dropping them on the carpet.

Her mouth left his to follow her hands, her lips first touching his exposed neck, then collarbone, then sternum, before she was stopped by the chain that held his jacket closed.

She lifted her gaze and met his, her eyes smoky with desire as her hands fumbled with the chain. He released her ass to help her with the chain, opening his jacket to expose the suspenders and cummerbund.

She spread his shirt as wide as the suspenders would allow and ran her hands over his pecs and down to his abs. There was reverence in her touch, and he blessed every painful hour of training that had given him this body that she clearly liked very much.

She straightened and grabbed his lapels, then walked backward, steering him to the couch where they'd kissed earlier. She turned him around so his back was to the seat, then removed the cummerbund and pushed him down onto the cushions.

He settled in as she filled his lap, straddling him. The silk robe slid open, revealing that she wore nothing underneath. His mouth found a nipple, and he sucked on it while his hands slid below the silk to cup her ass again.

He reached between their bodies, his knuckles brushed her clitoris as he unfastened his trousers. She purred as she reached into his briefs and took his penis in hand, stroking him from base to tip as he turned his fingers and focused his attention on her clit.

She met his gaze and spoke the first words they'd shared since stepping inside her apartment. "Can I have this, Carlos?"

He nodded, transfixed by the feel and sight of her hand stroking his hard prick. "Yours," he said, his breathing growing ragged. His brain cleared enough to add, "Condom?"

She smiled and reached into the pocket of the silk robe and pulled out a strip of condoms.

Really, what had he done in this life or the last to deserve this perfect moment? But he wasn't fool enough to second-guess. He would just take this—take her—and be thankful to the gods for smiling down on him.

Kaylea opened a packet and rolled the latex down his length, then she scooted up on her knees until her opening teased the head of his cock. He was usually one for more foreplay, but this...the suddenness of it was hot as hell. He'd explore every inch of her later.

She sank down on him, taking him deep in one perfect, slow, incredible slide. Seated as deep as he could go, he cupped a hand behind her head and pulled her mouth down to his. He kissed her as his hips thrust upward, grinding into her.

She sucked on his tongue and rocked her hips. Her tight pussy clenched around his cock, sending surging pleasure radiating from his core. "Kaylea." Her name was the only word he could form coherently. He said it with wonder, maybe. Or with awe. He couldn't be sure. It was his new mantra.

Kaylea. Kaylea. Kaylea.

Hot, dirty Spanish slipped from his lips, a stream of words that expressed pleasure, surprise, and all the things he planned to do to her tonight. With his mouth. His fingers. His tongue. His cock.

And she rode him. Rising on her knees, she slid up his shaft, then dropped down again. Sending more waves of pleasure, bringing him to the edge of oblivion. He cupped a breast and sucked on it, then switched to the other. He slipped a hand to where their bodies joined and wet his thumb in her arousal, then stroked her clit with it, rubbing the bundle of nerves in time with his thrusting hips.

She arched her back, the column of her neck a graceful curve as she faced the ceiling. The silk robe hung off one shoulder, exposing one breast while the other side was covered. The contrast of her dark skin and the orange robe along with the bounce of her bare breast and the imprint of the hard nipple through the silk fabric over the other was incredibly erotic.

His thumb worked her clit as he thrust into her. He watched her breasts and felt her clench around him as she let out a guttural sound. She gripped his open lapels and screamed with release, her body's quakes giving him permission to let go of the last shred of his control. His orgasm came hard, fast, and fierce.

This woman. This incredible woman.

She looked down at him, then lowered her head and kissed him, similar to how she'd kissed him in the street yesterday. Sweet. Soft. Easy. Like something she'd done a thousand times before. She raised her head, and he smiled up at her. "Well hello, Kaylea."

She laughed, and her smile deepened. "I'm *not* going to explain this to your XO."

He thrust his hips upward, enjoying the feel

of being inside her still, even if he was at fading half-mast. "Luckily, there is no need. None of his damn business."

Slowly, he rose from the couch, holding her, still inside her. She wrapped her legs around his hips. The suspenders kept his open pants from falling to the floor and tripping him. "I think I need to get you to a bed and get this damn uniform off so we can do this again, but more slowly the second time. And third and fourth."

He carried her across the living room and into her bedroom, where he deposited her on the bed. He slipped off the condom and went into the bathroom to clean up, then returned to the bed and her.

He stripped off his clothes and climbed above her, settling his hips between her thighs. Her legs wrapped around him, her calves resting on his ass. She smiled up at him, brushing his hair off his forehead. "Brains, brawn, and badass. I like you, Carlos. A lot."

"I like you too, Kaylea. And I'm about to show you how much. Again."

5

Kaylea felt languid. Content. Perfectly, wonderfully, gloriously fucked. She rolled over and faced the man in her bed, who'd delivered two orgasms already. Carlos Espinosa. Damn, he was hot. And fun. And smart. And badass in the best ways possible.

And when he spoke dirty Spanish in her ear? She could come again just thinking about it.

He smiled down at her, looking as content as she felt. "What are you thinking about?"

"I'm thinking about how much I like this. Like you."

His lips brushed over hers. "I think you're incredible. And not because of tonight—although you're incredible when it comes to sex too." His hands stroked her bare ass under the blankets. She loved the possessive touch. She could get used to this.

Except he was leaving. Not next week or next month. Saturday. It was officially her least favorite day of the week.

She stroked his cheek. His skin was smooth.

She knew Special Forces were allowed to grow beards as a way to connect with locals. Relaxed grooming standards, it was called. Up until yesterday, Carlos had sported a full beard. She'd been surprised to see his smooth jaw tonight, but she had no complaints. He was hot as hell bearded or shaved.

"I want you to know...I didn't ask you to be my date tonight because I was expecting this. I didn't have an ulterior motive. I just...like you. And when I realized I needed someone with me at the party, you were the first person I thought of."

A smile slowly spread across his face as his hand moved over her butt, across her back, and up to her neck. His mouth hovered an inch from hers. "And I want you to know I didn't accept with any notion or intent to end up here. You wanted help, and I wanted to give it. Freely, without hopes or expectations beyond a night out with a woman who impresses the hell out of me."

His words warmed her already hot body.

"Are you sure you need to leave Djibouti on Saturday?"

He laughed. "Unfortunately yes. Until yesterday, I was counting the days until I could go home."

"And now?"

"Now I want more. I want you. I want to see where this can go."

She wanted that too. But it was impossible. "I can't make promises beyond Saturday. My work is here, until the CIA and the State Department send me somewhere else."

"We can email. FaceTime. Talk on the phone."

"Phone? What is this thing you speak of?" She laughed at her own joke as her hand ran down his chest. "I really like you, Carlos. I like this. But you know what I am. What my life is. If you were going to be in Djibouti for a few more months, it would be different. Maybe we could carve out time to be together and see where this is going. But I can't see that happening once you're stateside. Who knows where they'll send you next, and who knows where they'll send me? Our schedules may never sync again. I'm just sorry we didn't try this sooner."

His eyes showed disappointment as she spoke, even as he pulled her closer. "I don't want to let you go, Kaylea. We could be amazing together."

She stroked his smooth jaw. "We *are* amazing together, tonight. Now. But I'm afraid that's all I can give." Her hand went lower, over his abs, until she stroked his penis, which thickened with attention. "I'm impressed," she said in a husky voice.

He nipped at her ear and ran his lips down her neck. "It's what you do to me. I'm too old to have this many erections in one night. But being naked with your hands on me, how can I not be hard?"

Her laugh was bittersweet. God. This man. This night. It was too good even for fantasy. If someone asked her to describe her perfect date, she wouldn't ever have dared to imagine anything this good.

He kissed her neck, lightly sucking. Not enough to give her a hickey, but part of her wanted him to mark her body as his, even if it was juvenile. Her dark skin hid hickeys well, and she could always wear a headscarf.

She wanted to be his. For more than one wild night.

They made love slowly this time. She didn't think she had another orgasm in her, but he proved her wrong, coaxing it out of her first with his fingers, then with his cock, and finally with his mouth.

Again, she was in a languid stupor. Thoroughly fucked and the happiest she'd been in years.

"Give me an email address," he said. "A way to reach you when I'm back in Kentucky. So we can communicate without going through the embassy. An email address that's permanent and secret."

"What makes you think I have email not connected to the embassy?"

He gave her a knowing look. "You have a way for close friends and family to stay in touch that isn't part of either of your jobs. You protect it like you protect yourself—always scanning for bugs when you enter a room or vehicle. I'm guessing you have an email address or phone number that's your most precious possession, because it keeps you in touch with your friends and family and reminds you of what you're protecting in this messed-up world. I want that number or address. I want to be able to contact you and know the communication is personal. Private."

He was right. She did have an email address. One she could access from anywhere. One she was extremely careful with because at times it was her only safe link to those who mattered to her. But if she gave it to Carlos, how would she be able to move on from him when their jobs kept them apart and he gave up and found another woman to lavish orgasms upon?

She couldn't hope for more with him, because more was impossible in her world. Especially with a Special Forces operator. She could fall for an embassy officer or other coworker, but no, she had to go for the badass soldier. What were the odds they'd find themselves in the same country again for any length of time?

They both loved their jobs. They'd both worked too hard to give their work up on the off chance that this relationship might go somewhere. She knew that better than anyone and had the ex-husband to prove it.

"Please, Carlos, can we just enjoy what we have tonight? You don't need to be back until morning. We've got hours left to enjoy this. Each other."

He held her gaze for a long moment and then said, "We can have tonight. But if you won't give me an email address or phone number by Saturday, you need to know I won't take your call on Sunday."

She could tell from the tone of his words he meant it. "Why?"

"I would happily spend the next year waiting for you, Kaylea, as long as I know I'm going to have you. But I don't do well with maybes, and I won't wait without a promise that we'll give this a try. To do that, we need to be able to communicate. I need to be able to email you and ask you how you're doing. You need to be able to respond as my lover and not a diplomat. If you won't give me a way to communicate that's safe for you, then you won't be giving us a chance, and I need to accept that starting on Sunday.

"I have a job with the Army that's dangerous. To do that job, I need a clear head. I can't be pining for you and keep my focus as I'm learning about the next latest and greatest explosive that can fuck up my world.

"I learned early on—after I made it through the Special Forces Qualification Course—that I need to compartmentalize to keep my focus. There is a crap ton of shit I need to know as an engineer and if I can't focus, the structure I'm building could collapse, or the one I'm destroying could take me with it. For me, compartmentalizing means shutting off relationships that aren't working before they get in my head." He ran his fingers over her cheekbone and down her jaw. "Waiting to hear from you will get in my head. Wondering if I'll hear from you, and *not* hearing from you, won't be good for my peace of mind. So, you have five days to make your decision. I'm part of your life and we see where this goes, or I'm not. But regardless, we have tonight."

She hadn't considered how uncertainty could mess with his mind, but he was right. And it would mess with hers too. She could easily see spending months trying to decide if she should call him when what she needed to do was let him go. For his sake. For her sake. She was a CIA case officer and a diplomat. Either job could call her to a different post, and one of her jobs could get her killed.

"We'll have tonight, then." She pushed him back on the bed, kissing him. She needed a lifetime worth of kisses tonight.

His hand cupped the back of her neck and started to slide upward, but then stopped. "Can I...run my fingers through your hair?"

It took her a moment for his words to sink in. As a Black woman, her hair had been subjected to the touch of strangers without permission since she was a child. It was a strange, uncomfortable thing to have strangers assume the right to touch. And here was a lover asking permission when she'd given him free access to her body. But Carlos Espinosa didn't take anything about her for granted, and that was a first in her experience.

"Please," she said. "Please, touch me everywhere."

"Yes, ma'am," he said. And then the man proceeded to give her a fourth orgasm of the night.

At oh four hundred, she walked him to her apartment door. They'd slept a few hours, and he needed time to drive back to base, return the SUV, and maybe grab another hour of sleep before he needed to report for duty at oh seven hundred. She was naked, and he was dressed in his blue mess uniform, ready to do the most glorious walk of shame Camp Citron had ever seen. She kissed him, gripping his lapels as if she didn't want to let him go.

"Give me your email address," he whispered against her lips. "So we can do this again. And again."

She shook her head. "You're right. We need to accept that this is all we get."

"It doesn't have to be this way."

"I can't see any other way. Not without one of us sacrificing who we are. And what I like about you and what you like about me is…who we are."

He smiled. "I'm also a big fan of your body."

She laughed. "And you have the most perfect body I've ever had the pleasure of licking."

And oh, how she'd licked him… Memories of tonight would feed all his fantasies in the future.

He placed a finger under her chin. "You have until Saturday to change your mind."

She said nothing, just kissed him. Finally, after a long interval, the kiss ended and she said, "Goodbye, Carlos."

He looked into the eyes of a woman he could easily fall in love with. He couldn't say goodbye. Not after what they'd just shared. "Thank you for this night, Kaylea."

Her door clicked closed behind him, and he heard the throw of the dead bolt. He took a deep breath and headed down the hallway to the stairs.

Holy hell. What an amazing night.

He fully suspected this night would take on mythic proportions in his mind. But there was no need to exaggerate the connection or the perfection. It had been spectacular on every level. Except the part where they'd have no repeats.

He had a few days to convince her. He'd be working during the day, but at night, he could call her cell phone. He still had that number, even if it was a work phone.

He plucked his cell from his pocket and texted her: *I miss you already.*

The dots appeared to show she was composing a message. He paused as he descended the stairs to the ground floor, waiting for her reply. At last the message came: *I think you've ruined me for other men.*

He grinned and texted a reply: *Good.*

He resumed walking. She'd come around. They could have it all.

His phone vibrated in his pocket, and he pulled it out. *Do you have to be so damn perfect? I'm pretty sure five orgasms is a world record.*

He texted back: *Only five?*

But damn, it was insane how her body had responded to him. How his had responded to hers.

Yes. She'd definitely come around. She'd give him a cell phone number or email address, and they'd get by with sexting until the next time they could be together. Kaylea Halpert was it for him.

Brainy, beautiful, and badass. And the best sex he'd ever had.

He reached street level and left the building, strolling down the quiet street in the dark hour before dawn as the waning crescent moon rose in the sky.

He'd never been in Djibouti City this time of night before. Hell, he'd barely spent time in the city at all. He wondered what it was like for Kaylea to call this place home. The city was darker than an American city would be at the same hour, but the moon was bright enough to light his way as he headed to the SUV. Surreal that this postdate walk was happening in Djibouti, on a deployment. Never in his wildest fantasies had he imagined anything like this.

He'd hooked up with women on base before when deployed, but quickly learned it could be awkward to then have months together in the same place if it didn't mean anything. For this reason, he hadn't had a sexual encounter while deployed in years.

He hit the Unlock button on the key remote. The lights didn't flash nor did the vehicle make a sound. Thank goodness for cautious mechanics in the motor pool who disabled these features that were fine in the US when picking up groceries, but not so great when driving a military-owned vehicle in a foreign country with hostile neighbors.

He reached the door and pulled it open. A sharp pain lanced across the back of his neck.

He pitched forward and hit his head on the top of the open doorway. Muscle memory kicked in and took control. He jabbed backward with his elbow, hitting a chest, while his other hand fisted and snapped up, over his shoulder, connecting with a face.

His hand brushed against a metal bar—the object used to hit him. He grabbed the bar and swung around with it in a tight grip.

A blow landed on his face as the bar connected with his attacker's side. A second man grabbed him and pulled him away from the vehicle, bringing the fight into the open street. A third man yanked the bar from his hand as another blow hit his face.

He was unarmed and surrounded by three very large, very angry men.

Kaylea stared at her phone. *I miss you already.* His text pretty much summed up what happened in her heart the moment the door clicked closed behind him. How could she face the coming empty months now that she'd had a taste of what could be?

He'd been so frank about how he felt; it was refreshing. The man didn't play games.

Sergeant First Class Carlos Espinosa. Special Forces Senior Engineering Sergeant. His rank, his name, his title, she'd known those for months. But now she knew the man, the Puerto Rican soldier who served his country with honor and the lover who blew her away with his passion.

How could she let him drive away into the night without giving him the one thing he'd asked for? He wanted a chance at a future, and the truth was, she wanted it too.

It was only impossible if she refused to give them a chance.

She couldn't send him the email address using her embassy account, and she couldn't tell him over a cellular or landline phone. The reason the email address was secure was because it wasn't in any system connected to her public identity. And he would need to set up a similarly private account to contact her. It was the only way.

She needed to tell him in person. Maybe he hadn't driven away yet, or maybe she could catch him on the way to the base.

She glanced down at what she wore. She'd donned underwear and her robe after he left, but that was all. Djibouti was not a place where a woman could run down into the streets in a silk robe. Not even at four a.m.

She darted into her bedroom. The nearest item of clothing was the gown she'd worn earlier, still on the floor where she'd dropped it when she stripped earlier. She tugged it over her head and reached for the shoes.

No. She couldn't run down the street in stilettoes—not if she actually wanted to catch up to him. She pulled on the knee-high boots, smiling at how ridiculous they looked with the dress, but Carlos liked the boots, so he'd enjoy her choice in footwear.

She grabbed her keys and ran out the door. She locked her apartment, cursing the precious seconds it took, but if she had to drive halfway to the base to catch him, she couldn't leave her home unlocked. Her diplomatic immunity meant police couldn't enter her apartment, but agents of espionage didn't exactly follow international agreements when it came to diplomats.

She was halfway down the stairs when she remembered she'd left her cell phone in her bedroom. She stopped short, then continued down the stairs at a run. If he was gone already and she had to drive after him, she'd run back upstairs and grab the phone. She could even text him and ask him to pull over. But she was hoping to catch him before he drove away. To surprise him. She wanted to see the look on his face when he realized why she'd come after him.

She reached the street and headed in the direction of where he'd parked, and halted in her tracks. Something was off.

The SUV was there. The driver's door hung open. But there was no Carlos.

The back of her neck tingled. This wasn't right.

Where was he?

She crouched low behind a large van and circled around to get a better view of the street beyond the military-owned SUV. She spotted Carlos, and ice shot down her spine. Two men held his arms while another punched him in the face and stomach.

The men had other weapons too—AK-47s, rebar, and handguns. She couldn't just charge them. It would likely get her or Carlos shot.

Did they know Carlos was a Green Beret? Or had he been targeted because of her? Had her cover been blown?

She needed to rescue Carlos, but her gun

was inside her apartment. Along with her damn phone.

Fuck.

Another blow landed on Carlos's temple, and his head slumped, slack, with his chin touching his collarbone. Was he unconscious or faking?

The men holding his arms dragged him down the road to an open Jeep. They bound Carlos's hands and dumped him in the backseat. One man climbed in beside him while the other two men climbed in the front.

The Jeep pulled away from the curb, tires squealing on the road. An object was tossed from the open vehicle right before it turned the corner and disappeared from her sight.

She darted down the road to see what they'd thrown and which direction they'd go at the next block. She saw the Jeep careen to the right as she spotted the tossed item. Carlos's phone. She scooped it from the ground—maybe she could use it to call Camp Citron—but no, it was shattered.

Damn.

No time to run upstairs to grab her own phone. She had to go after the Jeep, find out where they were taking him.

As she ran back toward her building to get her car, she spotted another item in the road. A car key. Could it be Carlos's key?

Please oh please.

She grabbed the key and jumped into the driver's seat. Tears sprang to her eyes as the engine started. This bit of luck could be the difference between Carlos living and Carlos dying.

She made a U-turn as she pulled out onto the street and skidded into the turn to follow the Jeep. She would find them. She would do whatever it took to free Carlos. And then she'd give him her email address.

Carlos's head throbbed. He hated letting them take him, but it was easier to pretend to pass out than to fight three armed men with only his fists, and he was more than a little curious about why they'd jumped him.

The best way to find out was to go along.

The men spoke Arabic and clearly assumed he did not. They speculated that Carlos was conscious, and one made threats in English in an attempt to test him. In Arabic, they insulted his manhood, while the one who'd taken Carlos's blows complained about his broken nose and painful jaw.

Carlos hoped he broke the asshole's jaw too.

Their conversation turned to their wait outside Kaylea's apartment. Apparently, they'd been waiting for him to leave the entire time he'd been there. The assholes called Kaylea disgusting names and expressed regret that they hadn't been able to grab her as well. It seemed they had already agreed on who would have gotten to rape her first if she'd accompanied Carlos to the street.

If Kaylea had been with him, these men wouldn't have lived long enough to touch her.

What did they want? Was this about Kaylea's work for the CIA, the sheikh's unwelcome interest in her, or could it somehow be about him? Did they know he was part of a Special Forces A-Team?

The road grew more and more rutted, and Carlos assumed they'd reached the outskirts of the city, making him wonder where they were taking him.

"Go faster," the man next to him in the backseat said. "We've only got thirty minutes to get there. We won't get paid if we're late."

Late for what?

The words confirmed the men had been hired for a one-off job and they weren't regular employees of whoever had ordered his abduction.

"It's not our fault we're late," the driver said. "It's the pig American's fault. He spent too much time fucking the whore. We should have moved on the apartment hours ago and taken them both."

They'd already argued this point. He gathered they hadn't stormed the apartment because they'd been ordered to be stealthy. Kaylea's diplomatic status meant a host of problems would come raining down if they were caught in the act of abducting Carlos from her apartment.

"Fault doesn't matter," the man in the front

passenger seat said. "He will miss the boat. The weapons will go to the Houthis without the American soldier to parade in the streets, and we won't get paid."

What the fuck?

A shipment of weapons was being sent to the rebel group in Yemen, and Carlos was meant to be part of the package?

Now he really needed to know where they were going. The man mentioned a boat, which was the most efficient way to get weapons to Houthi rebels. A quick sail across the Gate of Tears, and they were in Yemen, but a drive out to the Obock region, where the strait was located, was about four hours from Djibouti City. No way they could get there in thirty minutes, so there must be another port they were taking him to.

The man in the seat next to him suddenly punched Carlos in the ribs. "If the swine hadn't left the party before we could grab him, we'd have our money, the girl, and we wouldn't have spent hours on the street in the city."

So, they'd been tasked with grabbing him before they left the party, but he and Kaylea had skipped out earlier than expected. Al-Farooq's palace was located on the water. The aerial view Kaylea had shown him included a sizable dock, the kind that could support a mega yacht—or a small cargo vessel.

But why would a Saudi businessman support Houthi rebels? Saudi Arabia was currently leading the campaign of airstrikes on Yemen in support of the ousted president. The

US was currently allied with Saudi Arabia's coalition.

Was al-Farooq a traitor to his country, or was he playing some other sort of long game?

But then, Kaylea had said al-Farooq was owned by Bratva, and Russia was aligned with Iran, while Iran sided with the Houthis. Kaylea had confirmed the Russian she'd been introduced to was Radimir Gorev. The oligarch was involved in a number of power plays on the continent, including backing a coup in DR Congo that Carlos's team had squashed last week.

Gorev played long games. Was al-Farooq yet another pawn Gorev hoped to crown and control?

Carlos wanted to open his eyes and see if he recognized landmarks on the road to al-Farooq's palace, but didn't dare. As long as these men thought he was unconscious, he had a better chance of taking them out.

They drove for at least another five klicks over pitted roads. One of the men made a phone call, telling the person on the other end they were on their way and to hold the boat. He hung up, grumbling that the man made no promises and the driver needed to hurry.

Boat or no boat, Carlos was certain al-Farooq would pay and pay well for an American Special Forces operator. But of course, al-Farooq would have to know Carlos was Special Forces. Kaylea had been required to provide his name and rank in her RSVP, but she'd specifically left out the part about him having a Special Forces tab, and green berets weren't worn with blue mess uniforms, nor was cover worn inside unless he was carrying.

Did al-Farooq know what he was?

Transporting an abducted American soldier to Yemen before Camp Citron rained Hellfires down on the sheikh could prove a problem, which explained the plan to have a boat ready to go before Carlos could get comfortable in his prison.

But first Camp Citron would have to know he'd been taken. He wouldn't be AWOL until oh seven hundred, which was a little over two hours from now. Of course, Kaylea might notice his car on the street, but if she left her building through the parking garage, she'd exit on a different street. She wouldn't see. Wouldn't know. Couldn't sound the alarm.

He had to face it, he was on his own, and his best odds lay in taking out these three before they reached al-Farooq's palace, or as Kaylea had implied, the Gates of Hell.

Abandon all hope, ye who enter here.

He would not abandon hope. He would escape. He'd take out these fuckers. He'd stop the shipment of weapons. And when he was done with that, he'd convince Kaylea there was hope for them as well.

He figured he had less than ten minutes until they reached the gate. He was biding his time, looking for the right moment to strike, when the driver let out an alarmed shout a moment before something slammed into the side of the Jeep.

The Jeep swerved, and the ground beneath the wheels got even bumpier. They'd been hit and were being run off the road. Carlos sprang into action. He wrapped his bound hands around the neck of the captor next to him and gave a sharp twist.

One down, two to go.

A glance at the driver showed the man slumped over the steering wheel. Blood spurted from his neck. A small silver piece of metal jutted from the wound. Was that a throwing star?

The vehicle slowed even as it swerved, the driver's body holding the wheel in a sharp turn. A figure in a blue and green dress ran alongside. She leapt forward, one hand grasping the bar above the door as the other yanked the driver from his seat. She then gripped the bar over the door with both hands and launched herself into the front, feet first. The heels of her kickass black boots aimed straight for the head of the man in the passenger seat. The man flipped out the opening on his side, his head hanging down with his legs still in the vehicle. Kaylea gave another shove, and he slipped off the seat, curling under the moving vehicle. The rear wheels of the Jeep bounced over the man as Kaylea settled in the driver's seat and hit the gas.

She was wearing the beautiful, airy gown she'd worn last night, her corkscrew curls still in the braid and puffy corkscrew crown ponytail she'd worn to the party and during all the hours he'd made love to her.

"Holy fuck. That was awesome." His voice was reverent. The word awesome used for its true meaning.

She glanced over her shoulder and smiled at him. "Oh, you're awake. Did you have a good nap?"

He snickered as he grabbed a knife from the dead man and cut the zip tie, then took the man's AK-47 before he shoved him out of the vehicle. He climbed into the front and settled into the passenger seat. "I dreamed of an incredible avenging angel who came to rescue me."

The Jeep's tires returned to the main roadway, and he cupped a hand behind her neck and pulled her to him, kissing her fast but deep.

"You're welcome," she said, her voice a bit breathy before she returned her focus to the rutted road. "Let's get you back to Camp Citron, Sergeant."

Before she could turn the wheel to make the required U-turn on the dark, empty road, he said, "No. We need to keep going."

"Why? What's going on?"

"There's a boat full of weapons intended for Yemen—to arm Houthi rebels. They'd planned to put me on that boat. It's supposed to leave in less than ten minutes."

"Fuck," she said.

"Yeah."

"We're on the road to al-Farooq's palace," she said.

"Yes. My guess is that's where the boat is. Give me your phone—I'll call Camp Citron.

Maybe they can scramble a Blackhawk to track the boat."

"Fuck," she said again.

"No phone?"

"No phone. I left it in my apartment."

He glanced at her dress and boots. He couldn't help but grin. Those boots were hot. "How did you know to come after me?"

"I didn't. I ran down to the street because I had to tell you something. I was shocked to see three guys beating you up."

"I got a few good blows in before they surrounded me," he defended with a chuckle.

She patted his leg. "I'm sure you did, honey."

He laughed and leaned over and kissed her neck. "You are. So. Fucking. Badass." He pulled back and looked at her profile as she kept her focus on the road. "What did you run down to the street to tell me?"

She took her gaze off the road and faced him. "My email address."

Even though he'd hoped that was what she'd say, he wasn't expecting to hear the words. His chest bloomed with heat. She was his. They would make it work. "You won't regret it, babe."

"I know."

She pulled off the road less than a klick from the gate to al-Farooq's palace. "What's the plan?"

He put his hand on the back of her neck and pulled her to him, this time kissing her longer and deeper than he could when she was driving the Jeep. She kissed him back, and he tasted the desperation and fear she must've felt as she raced after his abductors to save him. He lifted his head. "Thank you for rescuing me."

"Anytime, soldier."

"Where did you get the throwing star?"

She reached down and slid her hand into her boot and pulled out a thin blade. "These boots are made for walking. And for doing serious damage."

"Your boots are filled with weapons?"

"And a few other treats, yes."

"The next time I make love to you, you're wearing the boots."

"Sure thing, cupcake."

He laughed again. This woman was full of surprises. "Okay, what have we got?" He had the AK-47 he'd taken from the guy in the backseat, but the men who'd been in the front seats had their guns on them when they left the vehicle.

She jumped from the driver's seat and circled the vehicle. He did the same on his side, carrying the AK. She flipped open a box in the back storage area. "We've got another AK, some handguns, and a few grenades. Not bad."

He glanced down at her boots. "What have you got on you?"

"Two blades. Some tranq darts and a blow gun. Tracking devices—but we'd need a cell phone or computer to receive the data—plus a few more odds and ends."

"If we put a tracker on the boat filled with

weapons bound for Yemen, Camp Citron could track it."

"Sure. We just need to let them know the URL for the tracker."

"Okay, then that's our goal. Find the boat, tag it. And go."

"We just need to get on the grounds, get to the harbor, and get near the boat with no one seeing us." She glanced down at her dress. "I'm not exactly dressed for this, but at least it's not a light-colored dress."

It was four forty-five a.m., and they had about an hour until sunrise, but it was getting light already.

"The aerial photo you showed me last night indicated the stone wall ends at the cliff's edge above the shoreline. If we can't find a good spot to climb the wall, we can go around the end." He hoped Kaylea wasn't afraid of heights, but after what he'd seen her do a few minutes ago, he was inclined to think she was Wonder Woman.

"Let's go, then."

They crouched down and darted between acacias until they reached the wall that circled al-Farooq's estate. The clock was ticking, but Carlos hoped the phone call had convinced the boat captain to wait a bit. After all, the promised delivery of an American soldier had to be worth the delay.

Think of the propaganda films that could be made if they dragged a soldier's body through the streets. It would be the ultimate false flag, an action to outrage Americans at the treatment of a soldier and to stir sympathy for the Houthis, at this proof that America was sending soldiers on off-the-books black ops. Because that was certainly how Carlos's presence in Yemen would have to be explained. But how would they explain the blue mess uniform? Not exactly an Army Combat Uniform. Although uniforms could be purchased, it was finding the authentic soldier to fill it that was hard.

At this point, Carlos suspected Kaylea had been invited to the party not because the sheikh was interested in her so much as who she could bring to him, but they would probably never know. Right now the priority was to stop more guns from being delivered into a brutal civil war. Arming Houthis wouldn't help the civilians caught in the crossfire, and Yemen was already on the brink of famine.

After less than two minutes, they got lucky. What looked like a completed wall in the aerial image wasn't quite so impressive on the ground. The wall height took a dramatic jump downward as it curved away from the road. It went from eight feet tall, to four feet, to two feet. Rocks piled nearby waited to be added to the short sections.

"Thank God for men who are so eager to show off their wealth, they don't wait until construction is complete," Kaylea said.

They scooted over the low barrier and crossed the grounds, sticking to the cover of trees where possible. They reached the hillside above the dock. Thanks to the slope of the property, it was only about twenty feet down to

the long pier that stretched out into the Gulf of
Tadjoura. And there, at the end of the dock, was
a large commercial fishing boat.

He'd bet his next paycheck there wasn't a
single fish in the hold.

What sort of weapons was the boat hauling?

Clouds rolled in, covering the thick crescent
moon, and they scrambled down the hill in the
weak cover the cloaked moon provided. When
they reached the dock, they crouched down in
prickly acacia shrubs and watched the activity.
At the far end, men loaded shrink-wrapped pallets onto the deck, and other men carried the
items below.

At the near end of the dock was a stack of
pallets, waiting to be loaded onto a dolly and
rolled down the dock. Carlos whispered in
Kaylea's ear, "Hand me a disk. I'll tag one of the
pallets here and let them load it on the boat.

She nodded and handed him a small disk.
"It's activated. Tuck it under the plastic, and
you're good to go."

He slipped through the shadows and
reached the stack of pallets. It only took a moment to insert the small disk under the plastic.
The clear disk disappeared under the layers, in-
visible to the casual or even not-so-casual
glance.

Perfect.

Now they just needed to alert SOCOM to
follow the signal. A phone would be a really
good thing to have about now. The sheikh had
his own cellular antennas. No fear that the
phone wouldn't work. If only they had one.

Too bad her boots couldn't hide a phone along with throwing stars.

He worked his way back through the shadows to where Kaylea hid. He'd settled in at her side when one of the men at the far end of the dock began pushing an empty dolly toward them.

It was a slow process of loading—apparently, Carlos's abductors didn't need to fear the timing as much as they'd thought. Or the men doing the loading were taking their time, hoping the abducted soldier would arrive soon.

They waited in the darkness as the men finished loading the boat. They wouldn't climb back up the hillside until after it was gone, or they might screw up everything by being spotted.

They could go back to the Jeep and drive to Camp Citron. Carlos would still make his oh seven hundred curfew. They'd have a lot of explaining to do, but the active tracker on the boat would go a long way to convincing his superiors to forgive Carlos for the loss of the SUV if they weren't able to reclaim it on their way back to the base.

Not that he was concerned SOCOM wouldn't believe his tale. Major Haverfeld and Captain Oswald were reasonable men, and they would take action once they learned one of their own had been abducted.

Shit. Pax and Bastian were going to tease the hell out of him. He had it coming after all the jokes he'd made over the years.

"Sweetheart," he whispered, "when we tell

the story about what happened this morning, would you mind telling people that I took out all three abductors?"

She snickered. "You're worried about your team teasing you?"

"Maybe a little." Then he draped an arm around her neck, pulled her close, and added, "I'm totally lying. I can't wait to tell everyone how you flew into the Jeep feet first and kicked the shit out of the prick in the front seat. And about the throwing star. You hit his *neck* while he was in a moving vehicle. I want every guy on base to know you're mine. Boots and all."

"I suppose I could confess I wasn't aiming for his carotid. I was aiming for his face, anywhere that would freak him out."

Movement nearby ended their conversation. He prayed al-Farooq didn't have dogs to protect the property.

After a long, taut moment, a bird took flight, and he let out his held breath.

Finally, the boat was loaded and it set out into the gray dawn. The two men who'd helped with loading pushed the empty dolly down the dock and rolled it into a shed, then walked the path that zigzagged up the hillside.

The Saudi businessman was nowhere to be seen, but Carlos hadn't expected to see him. He wasn't the sort to get his hands dirty.

"I want to check out that shed," Kaylea whispered.

Dawn was already lighting the sky, even if the sun hadn't officially risen yet. There would be no darkness to hide them as they crossed the grounds, so taking the time to inspect one shed wasn't a big deal.

Certain no one was around, they darted to the shed. Kaylea made quick work of the lock, with a pick she grabbed from her boot.

He really liked those boots.

Inside the shed was all that was to be expected for storage near a long dock into a sea that connected to the Red Sea and Gulf of Aden. Ropes, dollies, wheelbarrows, tools. And on the counter sat a phone.

Kaylea smiled and picked up the handset, then frowned to see it had no buttons. It was an intercom, probably connecting to the main house. "Dammit," she whispered.

"That would have been too easy, I suppose."

She frowned at the handset. "We'd probably find a dozen different landlines in the house. Even if al-Farooq uses cell phones for business, the service staff has to be reached somehow."

"You want to go into the house. To look for a phone."

"Pretty please?" She batted her eyelashes.

"No."

She sighed. "You're right. You're right. I know you're right."

He leaned down and kissed her fast and hard. "Let's get the hell out of here."

She was a little breathless as she said, "Yes, sir."

They set out together, this time heading down the shoreline. They would find a path up when they were no longer on al-Farooq's property. With daylight upon them, they couldn't take chances.

The steep cliff became a gradual slope, and they hiked up, away from the water. Kaylea produced a compass from one of the hiding places in her boot and gave him the bearing that would take them back to the Jeep.

"I need to get a pair of boots like those."

"If you do, you're wearing them when we have sex."

"Sure thing, cupcake," he said.

She laughed.

They made their way through the acacia. The Jeep was in sight. No one around. In minutes, they'd be back on the road. They'd drive straight to Camp Citron, and SOCOM could track the boat. They'd question the captain and find out what the hell they'd planned to do with an abducted soldier.

They were thirty yards from the Jeep, when he saw movement by the wall to the estate.

Motherfucker. A guy was holding a shoulder-fired rocket launcher. He fired, and a moment later, the Jeep exploded.

Kaylea saw the small rocket the moment before it was fired at the Jeep, and turned to run away as the boom sounded. The noise and wave of heat were enough to make her stumble, but she managed to stay on her feet, her hearing only slightly muted by the blast.

Beside her, Carlos also kept his feet. He took her hand and pulled her forward, urging her to run faster. She did, running flat out over the open terrain, running away from the Jeep, away from the palace. Their only hope was to run and hide and hope the blast had been noticed and help would come.

But it wasn't like the blast in Djibouti City that had been massive and heard for miles. This rocket had been much smaller. More of a bang than a boom. Plus the house was alone on a peninsula on the coast. For all she knew, there'd been blasting during construction of the palace and no one would bat an eye at the noise today. They couldn't count on any sort of cavalry. They were on their own.

She ran, her lungs aching as she pushed herself to run even faster, saving nothing for later.
But the ground and her boots weren't made for
this kind of running, and she rolled her ankle
on a rock and stumbled. Carlos was there to
pull her to her feet, and she ran again, ignoring
the pain.

She wasn't as trained as Carlos—few were—
but she was trained. She would do this. She
could do this. She didn't want to be the reason
he was captured. He could run faster. He was
holding back for her. "Go! Don't wait for me!"
She yelled the words, but they were muted to
her own ears and strangled by her panting
breath.

He ignored her plea and stayed by her side.

She ran with no destination in mind. They
were just trying to get away. Away from the
man with the shoulder-fired rocket launcher.
Away from the house.

But it was no use. A vehicle came barreling
toward them. This one a modern, short-wheel-
based Land Rover. More men with guns pointed
at her and Carlos. Bullets hit the ground in
front and behind her—the sharp crack of sound
barely penetrating her blast-fogged ears. These
weren't the lousy shots of poorly trained soldiers. They were warning shots. A command to
stop.

These men wanted to take them alive. If
they wanted to kill her or Carlos, they'd be
dead already. But that didn't mean they
wouldn't kill them. Just that they didn't *want*
to. Not yet, anyway.

She had no choice and collapsed on the ground. Unable to breathe. Unable to think. Unable to hear. Carlos was beside her, pulling her into his arms. "She's injured!" he shouted in English, his accent thick. Fully in character, even now.

Into her ear, he whispered, "Play along." She could just make out the words above her panting breath and the ringing in her ears.

She gave a slight nod. She couldn't draw attention to her boots—she wanted to keep them on—so she gripped her arm. "My shoulder!"

Four men poured out of the Jeep and surrounded them. Carlos spoke in Spanish and English, pleading for help for her, and she writhed as though in pain.

Once her breathing was under control, she could hear more, including the men's confused conversation in Arabic. None of them understood her injury. They'd been ordered not to shoot her or Carlos. Carlos was the one they needed, but they'd been ordered to take them both alive. The boss wanted the woman too.

For his part, Carlos pretended ignorance of Arabic. He worried over her fake injury, refusing to let her go. Finally, it was agreed—with their new captors speaking Arabic and Kaylea translating between her screams of pain—that Carlos would be permitted to carry her to the Land Rover.

They took the AK-47 and other guns, but their search of Kaylea was cursory given that she was in Carlos's arms and he refused to set her down. They were satisfied she had no phone or other weapons.

Once in the back of the Rover, he held her on his lap. She'd managed to produce very real tears—frankly, it didn't take much effort in this situation—and he stroked her back and spoke to her in English in his thickest accent. He swore no one would hurt her. He wouldn't let her go.

The Rover drove across the rocky ground, heading toward al-Farooq's estate. One of the men rode in the rear storage area now that she and Carlos had taken his seat.

It didn't take long before they once again passed under the gate to hell and rounded the circular drive, finally stopping directly in front of the grand arched doorway to the first dome, where al-Farooq stood.

⚓

Carlos added "amazing actress" to the list of Kaylea's attributes. He would swear she'd dislocated her shoulder if he didn't know the joint was perfectly fine. He was worried about the ankle she'd twisted, but she'd wisely avoided using that injury. It was vital she keep the boots on. As long as he could continue carrying her, no one would see her limp.

One of the men who'd taken them tried to reach for her to pull her from the Rover, but Carlos refused. He set her on the seat. Her arms remained locked around his neck as he lowered his legs to the ground, then scooped her up and turned to face their host.

As usual, al-Farooq did not look happy to see him. *Too bad, asshole. Kaylea's mine.*

She tucked her head into his neck and let out a soft whimper. "My shoulder hurts so much. And my ears. I can't hear anything."

One of al-Farooq's henchmen reached for her. She wrapped her "good" arm tight around Carlos's neck and let out a shriek. He jerked away from the man, holding her close. "Don't touch her!"

Al-Farooq barked at the man in Arabic, telling him to let Carlos hold her for now. The woman was a diplomat—with full immunity—and until they knew who was aware she was here, she was not to be harmed. If the police stormed the palace to look for her, al-Farooq—who did not have immunity—would face far too many questions and the woman would walk away scot-free, no matter that she'd been seen trespassing on his property.

Carlos was grateful al-Farooq didn't know he spoke Arabic, and he appeared to have bought into Kaylea's lie about not being able to hear, or at least hoped her sobs made it hard for her to focus on his words.

He guessed al-Farooq didn't know Kaylea was CIA, or he wouldn't be concerned about her diplomatic immunity. If he knew she worked for the Agency, she'd be dead already.

Carlos met the sheikh's gaze. "What do you want from us?" He kept the thick Spanish accent he'd used last night.

"Interesting you should ask me that when you were trespassing."

"I was brought here after your men abducted me in the street." Not exactly true, but close enough.

"A ridiculous lie by a soldier who wishes to cause trouble between our countries. Follow me." Al-Farooq turned and walked through the ornate arched doorway.

Carlos had no choice but to do as he said. In the entryway, Carlos couldn't help but notice the grand palace didn't look quite so perfect in the bright light of day. Dim lighting and candles had hid a lot of cut corners.

Similar to how the stone wall had looked finished in aerial view and from the road that ran along the front of the property, but portions of the wall that weren't visible to the casual observer would only be effective in keeping out toddlers.

Inside the front domed room in the full light of day, it was easy to see paint didn't reach the edges of the walls and the stained glass windows were merely colored glass—or plastic—with lines painted over it.

Yet the construction had clearly cost a fortune, so cutting corners on the final details seemed odd. Sheikh Rashid bin Abdul al-Farooq clearly had money, but perhaps not as much as he wanted the world to believe? That fit with Kaylea's belief the man was owned by Bratva. Had Bratva paid for this house? Was the man not a sheikh at all?

Why had he built this elaborate home in the

first place? He'd been positioning himself as a benefactor for poor Djibouti, but this made it look like the whole rich philanthropist image was a con.

Not that Carlos had believed he was a philanthropist, but trappings of wealth that didn't hold up under inspection definitely hinted at a con of some sort. And last night, everyone in politics and power in Djibouti had been to his home, paying homage to the tiny country's newest, richest expat.

"This way," the sheikh said.

The armed men followed behind Carlos, or he'd consider taking al-Farooq out before this went any further.

The man led Carlos down the corridor they'd merely crossed the night before, pausing for only a moment in front of the massive arched opening of the larger domed room. Carlos glanced into the ballroom and saw the dripping ice horse sculpture, now a third of the size it had been last night. Headless and legless, it was now merely an oblong ice block that wept water over the spread of food, which remained on the table.

The staff hadn't bothered to refrigerate the leftovers?

While last night there'd been air-conditioning to cool the packed room, now the space sweltered in the morning heat. The food would rot within hours if it remained on the table. What a disgusting waste.

They took a left down the long corridor that ran the width of the house, then a right once they were beyond the domed ballroom. This corridor was unfinished. They passed rooms that connected to the courtyard and pool area, which also appeared unfinished, before turning into another hallway.

Finally, the sheikh opened a door to a small bedroom-sized storage room. There was no window, cabinets, or shelves. The space was a simple rectangle with a drop cloth on the floor alongside dried-up paint cans, rollers, trays, brushes, and other tools.

"You will wait in here," al-Farooq said.

Carlos carried Kaylea inside. The armed men entered the room and took the tools but left the drop cloth. They left, and Carlos heard the click of the lock.

A two-sided dead bolt for a closet... Maybe the sheikh had intended this room to be a cell?

The moment the door closed, Kaylea held her finger to her lips as she had in her apartment last night. He set her on her feet, careful of the ankle that might be sore. She smiled, brushed her lips over his in a fleeting kiss, and pulled out a bug detector from the heel of one boot, along with the white noise/signal jammer she'd had in the city two days ago. She flicked it on, but it didn't make a sound. He guessed just the jammer was working. White noise, if someone was listening at the door, could raise suspicion.

It only took a moment to scan the room and drop cloth. He lifted her, and she checked the ceiling light fixture. He set her on her feet, and she nodded toward the air-conditioning vent above the door. He boosted her up again, and she scanned the vent first with the bug detector, then with her tiny LED light.

He lowered her to the ground, and she whispered in his ear, "All clear." She tucked the tools in their various slots in her boot.

He studied the heel where the signal jammer lived. The three-inch-thick arched block that narrowed only slightly from base to tip looked like layers of wood stained black. Once he knew what to look for, he could spot the compartment, but he'd never have guessed it was more than a joint between two pieces of wood if he didn't know otherwise.

He sat in the far corner, eyes on the door, and pulled her down so she was on his lap. They could talk quietly this way and watch the door. Plus it meant having her in his arms, and right now, he needed that. Regardless of all that had happened, they were both whole.

She shifted, getting comfortable, and his cock thickened. Not a full-on erection—their situation was too dangerous for his body to be that stupid—just enough to show he wasn't dead either.

He pressed against her, taking a moment of pleasure at the feel of his prick against her gorgeous ass. She really had amazing curves. "I haven't taken you from behind like this yet," he whispered.

"*Español, por favor,*" she whispered.

He grinned at the realization she spoke Spanish and hadn't told him last night. The things he'd said while making love to her...

He switched to his native tongue. "Fine. I want to bend you over the back of a couch or press you belly down on a mattress with your ass in the air and fuck you from behind until we're both blind."

"Yes, please," she whispered.

They would make love again. Last night was the beginning, not the end of this thing between them. "You still smell like sex," he said. "My scent is all over you."

"Do you like that? You've marked your territory."

"Very much. I want you to be mine and for everyone to know it."

She twisted her head and kissed his neck. Her chest rose as she took a deep breath, as though she was breathing him in. "I've got two blades in my boot, plus the tranq darts and other tools. I can pick the lock, and we can get out of here and find a phone."

Those might be the hottest words he'd ever heard. And she'd said them in Spanish. He nuzzled her neck. "I could fall in love with you, Kaylea Halpert."

Her body shook with silent laughter. "It's my middle name."

"What's your middle name? Kaylea?"

"No. My email address. It's my middle name and the year of my birth."

"And what's your middle name?"

She kissed him, her tongue sliding between his lips. Sweet and seductive. Far too hot for the circumstances, but somehow just right. "I could tell you, but I like the idea of making you work for it."

He laughed. "I didn't work enough last night? Five orgasms, if I remember correctly."

"You did. And you do." She kissed him again. "I could fall in love with you too, Sergeant First Class Carlos Espinosa."

His arms tightened around her. Later, he'd get her middle name. Right now, they needed to plan their escape.

9

Kaylea studied the vent above the door. "I have an idea," she whispered. "The vent opening would be a tight squeeze for me, but from what I could see, the duct itself is industrial size—large enough to crawl through."

Given the massive front rooms of the house, the industrial ductwork made sense. There had to be a room-sized air-conditioning unit somewhere on the property.

Carlos said nothing. She shifted on his lap so she could see his face. He stared at the grate. "No way can I fit through that opening, not unless we bent back the metal and tore out drywall. We don't have the tools or time for that, plus I'm pretty sure there's a guard in the hall who would hear."

He was right. His shoulders were far too broad. Too much muscle mass. "I'd have to go by myself. You can put the vent back in place. If someone finds you alone before I can get you out, you can claim one of al-Farooq's men came and got me. Turn them against each other."

After a long silence, he nodded. "That plan buys us the most time, which is what we need more than anything. We pick the lock to go out the door but find a guard in the hallway, we'll end up back in here without your tools."

"We need to hurry, though. They might be getting a real cell ready and come back and move us—or separate us—at any time." She stood from his lap and crossed to the door, making sure her steps were silent on the bare plywood floor.

Why had al-Farooq hosted a party last night when his palace was so far from being completed? The aerial photos she and Carlos had viewed last night had shown the swimming pool and landscaping under construction. She'd assumed the images had been taken weeks ago and the party would be in the gardens, but it had been confined to the main rooms of the house, and she'd caught glimpses of the incomplete pool and gardens on the way to this room.

As far as she could discern, the purpose of the party had been nothing more than to show off his wealth and convince other nations he was a great benefactor of Djibouti. But his display would've been more impressive if he'd waited a few months and hosted Djibouti's politicians and most of the resident foreign diplomats when house and grounds were complete.

She whispered these thoughts to Carlos in Spanish as she inventoried the supplies hidden in her boots. She gave him a thin blade to hide in the lining of his jacket, and a small file. "Use this to sharpen your cuff links. The shirt studs too, if you can."

He nodded and tucked both items into the liner of his jacket.

Carlos would have to replace the grate and screw it back to the wall once she was inside the duct, but while he could reach the grate itself, the screws were an inch beyond his fingertips. Without a word, he demonstrated how they could work around this by folding the canvas drop cloth into a thick square. Standing on the cloth, he could just reach the screws.

Ready to make her escape, she pulled his face down to hers and whispered, "I hate leaving you. They'll hurt you when they find you in here alone."

His lips brushed hers. "I'm terrified of what will happen to you if they catch you." His kiss was deep—almost savage in its intensity. He raised his head and said, "Do whatever you have to do to save yourself. Even abandon me."

She held his gaze. Finally, she whispered, "You too. I'll find a phone, call SOCOM, then I'll find a way to get you out of here."

Carlos bent down, and she climbed on his shoulders. She pulled a tiny, flat multitool from a sleeve in her left boot and inserted it into one of two screws that held the vent to the wall. New construction made it easy to remove, and she handed the rectangular grill to Carlos, who quietly set it on the floor by his feet.

He rose to his full height again, and she hoisted herself into the opening. He pushed up on the backs of her thighs so her legs wouldn't bump the wall and cause a noise. As she'd seen with the flashlight, the duct itself was much wider than the opening, but she had to get through the short rectangular joint without making noise first.

She'd always enjoyed her curves, which included a generous round butt, but the feature was also the largest circumference on her body and might not fit through the opening. For Carlos, the problem was his muscular shoulders. For her, it was her fat ass.

The metal edge of the duct scraped her dress as her rear was forced to reshape as if she was Play-Doh being squeezed through the Fun Factory, but she made it through with very little noise thanks to Carlos's patient, steady hands that pushed her carefully from behind.

She crawled forward into the larger metal tube perpendicular to the six-inch-long rectangular joint. Once she was fully in, she crawled backward until her head could poke into the joint and she could see into the room.

She met Carlos's gaze. She couldn't speak. They were too far apart—any words he could hear could also be overheard by others. So she pressed the tips of her fingers to her lips and blew him a silent kiss.

He replaced the grate in the opening. His eyes were intense as his gaze held hers in silence. She handed him the tool, and he fastened the two screws, then passed the tool back to her.

His fingers slipped through the square holes in the grate, and she brushed them with her lips, then crawled forward as silently as she could in the long, hot metal tunnel.

⚜

C arlos paced, whispering in Spanish and pausing as though listening to Kaylea's response. Anything he could do to buy time and convince the guard in the hallway there were still two people in this room as he sharpened his cuff links and dumped the drop cloth back in the same disarray it had been in when they entered the room.

He tried not to worry about her, tried not to imagine what would happen to her if she was caught. Tried not to blame himself for bringing her here instead of getting her to safety, then finding a phone. It had been his call to come here, his call to go after the boat. Deep down, he knew she wouldn't have made any other choice, but that didn't mean he wouldn't blame himself.

She *was* trained for this sort of thing. She wasn't Special Activities Division like Freya, but she'd been to The Farm. She knew what she was doing.

But still, he was terrified.

Her job was dangerous in a way that was different from his. When he went into combat, he knew there would be people literally gunning for him. Her job was fancy parties in palaces and recruiting agents for the CIA. The agents she recruited were the real spies. And her role in gaining their cooperation was a vital tool in the CIA's intelligence-gathering arsenal, and very dangerous should it be revealed.

If al-Farooq discovered she was CIA, he'd kill her on the spot. And right now, she was crawling through the guy's ventilation system like it was her own personal highway through hell.

Carlos paced and talked to himself and focused on what he would do the minute the door opened. He guessed Kaylea had been gone a full forty-five minutes when he heard the lock turn.

❧

The duct was an oven baking Kaylea alive. But being baked alive was better than what Carlos could be facing if al-Farooq or his henchmen found him alone. The idea of what he might be facing threatened to terrify her into paralysis, but that would mean he'd face that danger for nothing, so she shoved it aside along with the discomfort of the hot duct and the sweat that poured down her feverish skin.

Slowly, she crawled. Inch by painstaking inch, she moved forward, not daring to move faster or she might make noise that would endanger both Carlos and herself. Sloths and snails held speed records compared to her progress, but she wouldn't screw this up. Patience was key.

She told herself this was like performing an extra-long Surveillance Detection Route. How many hours of her life had she wasted driving

SDRs? After her lengthy training and nearly four years of covert work, way too many.

This was like that, just more miserable because she was cramped in a tight vent that had to be about three thousand degrees. The system was new, so it was relatively clean, but still, it was Djibouti, so there was dust. And razor-sharp edges of sheet metal at the joints. A thousand reasons to go slow, but her brain screamed at her to hurry.

The man she was falling for, the man she'd just shared an amazing night with, the man she was increasingly certain she wanted—*needed*—in her life, was counting on her. She wouldn't let him down.

At each intersection or grate, she stopped and listened for several minutes before determining if the room below was empty and which direction she should go. She aimed for the back of the house, figuring she'd be more likely to find al-Farooq's real operations center away from the lavish front public rooms.

He probably had a formal office in the front of the house too, but that wasn't where he'd keep his computer, not the one with real information on it, anyway. No, the front room would feature a big, heavy desk carved from some endangered rainforest wood, with nothing on the polished dark surface. The visitor's chair would be upholstered in something ridiculous and horrible, like a zebra pelt or dragon scales. Al-Farooq would invite ambassadors and diplomats, and ministers and presidents to his home, and they'd meet in the formal office, and he'd cut deals after revealing the kompromat his Russian allies had gathered on whichever victim was in the chair.

In a way, Kaylea was a different side of the same coin, recruiting people to her country's side in the intel wars, but she used bribes to persuade, not blackmail. Her assets were individuals deeply concerned about the actions of those in power in their homelands, and they were privy to information that could change things. Some were patriots; some wished to escape to America and saw gathering intel for the US as a path to freedom. They all had their reasons, and not a single one of them had been caught on video strangling a prostitute, as the Russians were fond of arranging.

What did they have on al-Farooq? Or was he just in it for money and power? He didn't have oil or a big family behind him. He was nobody, from nowhere, and he'd chosen Djibouti to be his seat of power because he would never be important in his home country.

Why poor Djibouti?

That question, Kaylea was fairly certain she could answer. It was the heart of the US military's operation in Africa. It was also where China was expanding their military operation. Everyone wanted a piece of Djibouti for its strategic importance. It was considered a country with a strong presidency but a weak government. Ripe for the plucking if you had the right kompromat.

The men who would face al-Farooq across his abomination of a desk would do what he required, and people far removed from wealth and power would suffer for wealthy men's moral failures, corruption, and greed.

Her view of humanity had turned quite bleak in the last few years, but she could back it up with receipts.

On the flip side, she'd also been on the front lines to witness acts of heroism, compassion, and valor. Citizens risking everything to stand up to their corrupt governments. People marching in the streets in open rebellion against dictators. Men and women sharing secrets with Kaylea in hopes of preventing atrocities. She'd seen all these things and had been filled with awe for the risks and sacrifices, while hating the necessity.

One thing was certain about al-Farooq and his ilk—they would do nothing good for Djibouti. He would make donations of food with one hand while he twisted the government to his own ends with the other, keeping the people hungry and trafficking in drugs, weapons, and slaves.

The whirr of the air-conditioning motor sounded, coming from the tunnel in front of her, sparking hope. She slowly crawled toward the sound. It would take time for the cool air to reach her, but relief from the relentless heat was coming her way.

She risked moving slightly faster. The white noise of airflow and the hum of the motor might cover her movement, and this was taking far too long. At last, cool air reached her. She paused, lay on her belly, and silently sighed with relief as the chill air touched her skin. She could stop here for a moment. She needed to think. To plan.

Now that she was at the rear of the house, she needed to drop out of the duct and into an empty room. Find a phone. Find weapons. Save Carlos.

After a short break, she resumed crawling, heading for a vent that extended to the right. She reached the opening and paused. She couldn't see anyone in the room, but her view was limited, and the room was furnished. Finished.

After several minutes, the air-conditioning shut off, removing the soothing white noise. Coming from the tunnel ahead of her, she heard voices. Not this room, but maybe the one next to it? The voices carried well down the duct.

Two men speaking in French. Her training was the only thing that stopped her from gasping when she recognized one of the voices. And it wasn't al-Farooq or one of his men.

If she'd had any doubt about this palace, it was now confirmed. She'd just entered the ninth circle of hell: treachery.

10

"Where is she?" Carlos shouted before al-Farooq had a chance to speak, let alone take in the fact that Kaylea wasn't in the room. "Where did your man take her?"

The sheikh's gaze darted around the empty room, then to his henchman, who stood in the hallway, before finally returning to Carlos. "What are you talking about?"

"I swear to you, Rashid"—he sneered the first name, underscoring the lack of respect—"I will kill you or any man who's hurt her."

Al-Farooq's gaze again darted around. "Where is she?" he snapped in Arabic.

Carlos felt a rush of satisfaction he couldn't show that the question was directed at the guard in the hall.

The guard protested, saying in Arabic he'd been guarding the room and no one had come in or out.

"What is he saying?" Carlos asked. "Is he telling you about the man who said Kaylea had to go with him so he could tend her shoulder? That he dragged her out of here?"

Al-Farooq turned a shocked look on Carlos, then back at his henchman, translating Carlos's accusation into Arabic. The man shook his head in a denial that worked in all languages.

"No one came! No one took her! I was guarding the door!"

The man stepped into the room, his gaze darting around. He looked up at the grate. He pointed. "She went through the vent!"

"Is he saying she somehow escaped?" Carlos asked. "How? The man who took her must've paid him. Or he left his post like a lazy dog." He lunged for the guard and grabbed his shirt. "Where is she? What did you do to her?" He punched him in the face before he could answer.

The man shoved at Carlos's chest, but he'd made a mistake in not raising his AK the moment Carlos went on the offensive. It turned into a brawl, and the man landed on the floor in an unconscious heap. Carlos toed him aside and fixed al-Farooq with a glare. "Where. Is. Kaylea?"

Al-Farooq glared back, clearly not knowing what to believe.

Carlos would've gone for the man's throat, but the noise of the fight had brought other armed men into the hall. A man shouted in Arabic followed by English, "Stop!" He wasn't as dumb as the first guard and pointed his AK at Carlos.

He froze and held up his hands in surrender. If he could convince al-Farooq he'd been betrayed, the men would be forced to divide and search for Kaylea. On one hand, this was bad, because they might actually find her. On the other, it would buy him time to find a way out.

"How do I know she did not escape through the vent?" al-Farooq asked in English.

Carlos glared at the man. "If she is raped by one of your men, I will castrate you both."

Al-Farooq lashed out, backhanding Carlos. "Prove to me she did not escape through the vent."

"How do I prove a negative?" Carlos glared at him. "The burden of proof is on you." Any argument to buy time.

"Then I will believe she went through the vent and you are lying."

"How? I can't even reach it. And it's a small vent. Have you seen Kaylea? No way would her chest and butt fit through that."

"You lifted her. Helped her through the hole."

"But how did I replace the grill and screw it back on?" He moved to the grill and made a show of having to jump to be able to reach it.

He jumped a second time and grabbed the grate, which he yanked from the wall, tearing out the screws from the drywall. He used the momentum from the jump to lunge for one of the new guards, swinging the grate. The sharp metal edges on the inside of the grill smashed into the head of the guard. His head snapped backward. His finger pressed the Kalashnikov's trigger as he dropped to the floor. The bullets drew a dotted line on the ceiling, then the weapon dropped from his slack grip. Blood seeped from a checkerboard of cuts on the man's face and temple, and his eyes closed. Unconscious or dead.

With more guards in the hallway holding AKs, Carlos couldn't hope to fight his way out of this now, so he had to be convincing and not waver in his story. He dropped the grate and held up his hands. "I'll ask one more time. Where. The fuck. Is Kaylea?"

Al-Farooq's gaze flicked to the two guards who lay unconscious on the floor.

The Saudi wanted Carlos alive, or no doubt he'd have a bullet in his back already. The man had probably spent the last hour trying to find another boat to take Carlos to Yemen. But Kaylea presented a different kind of threat to the businessman. "She's a diplomat, and everyone at the embassy knows she's here," Carlos said. "My CO and XO know I'm here. You're going to have a lot of uncomfortable questions to answer, so you'd better hope she's okay, because if not, the US is going to rain Hellfires on your ass."

A strange light filled al-Farooq's eyes, then it dimmed and he began shouting orders in Arabic. For the moment, he would believe Carlos and set others to searching for Kaylea and the traitor who'd taken her. But this was what he'd do even if he didn't believe the lie, so it did what Carlos needed most—it bought time for Kaylea to find a phone, and time for Carlos to remain among the living.

While one man set off to organize the search, another grabbed Carlos and bound his hands with a zip tie, this time at his back. He waited for the man to take the cuff links, but thankfully, they remained at his wrists, the sharpened edge right next to the plastic binding.

He was shoved forward through the door and down the hall, with two guards on his heels. They'd said nothing in Arabic or English about where they were taking him, and al-Farooq hadn't given instructions. But did it really matter? All the circles of hell were still hell.

Kaylea listened in horror as Stephen Walker, the American embassy's public diplomacy officer, spoke with…she wasn't sure who else was in the room, but it wasn't al-Farooq. The man's French had a decidedly Russian accent.

She tried to remember Gorev's voice from the night before, but they'd spoken in Russian, and even then only briefly.

"Why the hell did you drag me here?" Stephen said. "If she sees me, this is all over. I got her to bring the soldier to the party. I did my part. You promised me that was it."

"But she and the soldier left the party before we could take them. And then when the soldier was grabbed, he was alone. And yet somehow he got away, and he and the girl came here. Why? What did you tell her?"

"I didn't tell her anything," Stephen said.

"You must have, because somehow, she and the soldier ended up here. We found the vehicle the man was driving. It wasn't far from three dead bodies. Men who had been hired to grab the soldier. There is no way anyone—let alone a foolish woman—could have found and rescued him unless they knew the plan."

"Dead?" Stephen's voice had gone from uneasy to full on afraid.

"Dead. A snapped neck. A slit throat. The third had both a broken neck and crushed chest. Someone knew the ambush was coming."

"Impossible. Kaylea doesn't know anything. She's just a stupid party planner obsessed with shoes who can speak a few languages. She's pretty but not all that bright."

She smiled, feeling so very glad that no one had trusted Stephen with the truth about her double life. Only the ambassador and deputy chief of mission knew. Her cover was too perfect to blow it by telling more than the two men who absolutely needed to know.

That Cal and Carlos had guessed had been a surprise, but she'd revealed herself when she ran to Camp Citron to make a plea for a team to be sent to help Freya and Cal. And she'd made a mistake of spending time with Freya at Camp Citron—one she hadn't repeated—but both Cal and Carlos had noted it anyway.

"The soldier is in Special Forces, though, just like you wanted. He probably overpowered the guys. Maybe they took Kaylea and he went after them."

You just keep on underestimating me, asshole. I can't wait to bring you down.

Stephen's casual suggestion she bring someone from the base as her date hadn't been so casual after all. What would he have done if she'd accepted his original offer to be her date? But she could easily see how he could've steered the conversation, rethinking the offer and suggesting she needed someone from special forces.

And of course, she'd latched on to that idea with lobster claws. Had he guessed she was interested in Carlos, or had it just been dumb luck on his part?

She tried to remember if there was ever a time Stephen had met anyone on the A-Team. At once, it flashed in her mind. A few months ago, after nearly two dozen girls had been rescued from Etefu Desta's stronghold in Somaliland, they'd been brought to the base. Kaylea had made arrangements for a safe place for the girls to live while she and others worked to track down their families. Kaylea and Stephen had gone to the base to pick up the girls to bring them to their new temporary home, and Carlos and a few of the others had stopped in to say goodbye to the girls. She hadn't said more than hello to Carlos, and hadn't introduced him to Stephen, but maybe he'd seen her react when she saw him. The unexpected

Carlos sighting had triggered a rush of excitement.

There was no way to know if it was luck or cunning on Stephen's part, but given that he thought she was a twit, she was going to assume luck.

"I swear, Gorev, she doesn't know anything."

So the man he was speaking to *was* Gorev. The oligarch had owned Seth Olsen and, apparently, Stephen Walker.

"I've been monitoring her phone for months," Stephen continued. "She's a fool who receives a lot of cat pictures from her mom. She reads a lot and spends a stupid amount of money on clothes and makeup. And I *warned* you she and the solider planned to leave the party early. You should have grabbed them both before they left. This isn't my fault."

And that was why she didn't ever put her most private email address in writing in any form on a device known to be associated with her. She always knew someone might be listening. She'd just never expected it to be someone from her own embassy.

"Who at the embassy knows she's here?" Gorev asked.

"No one," Stephen said. "Her phone is still in her apartment. *I* didn't even know she was here until you told me."

"What about the soldier? Does anyone from Camp Citron know he's here?"

"He sent some text messages to Kaylea at four a.m. and hasn't used his phone since. The base can track the SUV, though. You need to destroy it. Far from here."

"Already done," Gorev said.

The air-conditioning unit kicked on again, and she couldn't hear the voices over the sound of the motor and the flow of air. Much as she wanted to stay and listen to what else Stephen had to say, this was a good time to try to find an exit in an empty room, while the unit provided cover noise.

She resumed her painstakingly slow crawl, her brain buzzing with all she'd learned. She took an offshoot duct, moving away—she hoped—from the rooms that were completed and occupied.

After ten minutes of slow crawling, she found a room that was empty and unfinished. It had a window and two doors. One could be a closet or bathroom; the other must lead to the hall. It was her best bet. It was time to get out of here and find a phone.

She put the small flat tool between two fingers—all she could fit through the square holes in the grate—and hoped the screws were in the same place and as easy to remove as the first had been. But in the end, she couldn't hold and work the screwdriver through the sharp grate. She would have to make noise and kick it out of the wall.

She crawled forward and positioned herself so her booted foot had room to extend and strike. She held her breath and counted to three, then kicked out behind her. The grate sprang free on one side. She kicked again at the other side, next to the second screw, and it popped off the wall.

In one movement, she scooted backward until her legs were out of the hole, and she had to get her butt through the Fun Factory again, but this time without help. At least gravity was on her side. She tightened her glutes and shoved through. She popped free in a rush and slid until she dangled from the hole by her hands. She felt the bite of sharp, raw metal and released the edge of the vent, falling to the floor, landing on both feet. The ankle she'd twisted sent a jolt of pain up her leg, and she collapsed.

She lay on her back, panting as quietly as she could manage, as she stared at the ceiling and prayed no one had heard her exit the ductwork. Dimly, it registered that her hands stung and were probably bleeding more than was recommended. Plus her ankle throbbed. But mostly she was glad to be out of the damn oven.

A s a combat engineer, Carlos knew construction and he knew demolition, and the more he saw of this house, the more he was certain no one planned for the construction on the back half to be finished.

Al-Farooq had gone down a hall to the right, but the guards had pushed Carlos to the left. After traversing several corridors, they entered a hall that was just a shell, like a set for a movie

that never went into production. There were
sections with studs but no drywall. Bare-bones
electricity. No plumbing. There weren't tools
lying around, like someone was going to come
back and finish the work, but there was debris
on the floor: piles of scrap metal and concrete.

Up above, the air-conditioning ducts were
exposed. Long silver tubing that ran the length
of what would be a hall, if there were drywall to
define it. "Where are you taking me?" he asked.
He dialed back on the Spanish accent, using his
normal voice in case they spoke English but not
well enough to understand the heavier accent.

"Shut up," one of the guards said.

Did that mean he spoke English, or just
knew basic phrases?

"Why isn't this house finished?" he asked,
projecting his voice. If Kaylea was near, maybe
she'd hear him. "What's with the garbage in the
middle of the house? This shit isn't leftover
from construction. There's no reason to drag
broken concrete into a house. It looks more like
rubble than construction debris." He came to
an abrupt stop.

It looks like rubble.

"Keep moving!" The guard shoved him
forward.

He darted to a pile of scrap metal and
looked at the jumble of wires and hydraulics—
complex machinery, torn to pieces. Hell, it
looked like a crashed drone. A cheap one, not
the kind the US military used, but a knockoff.

He glanced around the room, searching the
studs and structural beams. He looked in the

places where he'd place a charge if he were trying to take this building down. And he spotted them.

Carlos knew construction, and he knew demolition. And this house was set to blow.

11

Kaylea gave a silent prayer of thanks when she found an empty office with a computer on the third try. The only problem was, there was no phone, and the computer was password protected. She had a device that could get around that, and she plugged it into the USB port on the computer. The CIA had developed this little beauty, and it even had its own built-in satellite connection for use with computers without internet access. The technology cost more than she made in a year but had the potential to reap enormous rewards, intelligence-gathering-wise, like when Freya had used one during her mission weeks ago. She wouldn't be able to use the computer to message anyone, but the device would copy all the files and upload them to cloud storage she'd configured for just this kind of occasion. Might as well grab what she could.

As the files uploaded, she searched the desk to be certain there wasn't a phone or anything else she could use. Nothing but power cords and basic office supplies.

A sound in the hall sent her to the closet. She closed the door just as a man entered the room. He must've seen the files being uploaded on the monitor because he cursed and made a beeline for the closet. He yanked open the door, and she tagged him with a tranq dart using her tiny blowgun.

He jerked back, reaching for his cheek where the dart had planted, and dropped to the floor.

She jumped out of the closet and closed the office door, then searched the man—who, if she remembered correctly, was al-Farooq's secretary or administrator. Whatever title he held, he was al-Farooq's right-hand man and just as dirty as the sheikh.

He had a cell phone in his pocket. But it was dead. *Dammit.* There'd been a charging cord in one of the drawers. She could plug it in and call.

She heard voices in the hall.

Shit.

No time to hide the man in the closet. If anyone entered this room, she was toast. She slipped into the closet, leaving al-Farooq's aide on the floor just outside the door. She held the dead phone to her chest and listened to the voices in the hall. Al-Farooq and Gorev. They entered the office next to her. Their voices were clearer through the back wall of the closet. The walls were thin.

Cheap-ass construction in a hastily built and

incomplete palace. She felt like she was on the set of a Disney movie.

From the layout of the house, she suspected they were in the office where Gorev had been speaking with Stephen earlier. Where was Stephen now?

"What are you going to do with the soldier?" Gorev asked in Russian.

"Too late to put him on the boat as a gift for the Houthis. I tried to arrange other passage for him, but it's too risky now. We will leave him here. Let him feast with the children."

"And the girl?"

"She knows too much," al-Farooq said. "She can place the soldier here. She too will feast with the children."

"When you find her."

"She hasn't left the palace. It doesn't matter if she's found. She will die."

"Her remains will be recovered in the investigation. The Americans will want answers."

"The Americans will never know it's her. We will not let the FBI investigate. They are suspect. Their investigations are just a means to hide American crimes. Like they did with the explosion in Djibouti City."

Kaylea realized he was giving his version of future events. There'd been no findings yet by the FBI and wouldn't be for days. But now she knew the purpose of the blast in the city, how it would be used to frame the US, to show the FBI wasn't honest in their investigation when it implicated Americans.

They would probably claim it was someone

from the base. After all, the military had access to C-4. Stir anger against the Americans with their large military base.

Camp Citron was the front line in the US war on terror in Africa and the Arabian Peninsula. It was vital the US maintain good relations with the Djiboutian government. A bomb planted by a soldier in Djibouti City? That would seriously harm diplomatic relations between the US and Djibouti.

But what did al-Farooq mean by "feast with the children"? What children?

In the room next door, Gorev said, "We need to leave, to be far away from here."

"I need my computer."

"No. Everything must stay. Fewer questions."

Whatever was going down would happen soon. She needed to find Carlos.

The guards led Carlos to a pair of studs that would form a corner—if there were walls. C-4 implanted with a detonator had been mounted to the joint with the beam. One guard shoved Carlos to stand in front of the studs while the other held his AK pointed at Carlos's chest. "No moves."

The guard tied him to the post. After tying the knots, the guard inserted a scrap of metal into the straps that bound Carlos and turned them, like a tourniquet.

He glared at both guards but said nothing as

the straps dug into his arms and chest.

The guard with the AK stepped up to him. His lip curled, then he raised a fist and punched Carlos in the face. The second blow was worse than the first.

He got the feeling these men were angry because of what Carlos had done to the two guards in the storage room. They wanted to cause him pain, but pain meant he was alive, so he'd take it.

"We should shoot him," the guard who'd tied him up said in Arabic.

The other man shook his head. "No bullet holes. Al-Farooq's orders."

Carlos refrained from looking up at the C-4. He didn't want these guys to know he understood what they were saying. One thing was certain, if Carlos was still tied to this post when the C-4 went off, there wouldn't be enough of him left to find bullet holes. But it was possible the two guards didn't know about the C-4.

The guard with the AK stepped back, raised the butt of his rifle, and said in English, "Enjoy your nap."

The weapon smashed into his temple, and the world went black.

12

Freya stepped out of her office in SOCOM headquarters, gripping the picture of the memorial wall at CIA headquarters in her hand. She couldn't believe she'd done it. She'd quit. And she felt...light. Alive.

She couldn't wait to tell Cal, but he was working with the trainees, trying to fit every last bit of lesson time into the limited days they had left in Djibouti. Maybe she should have waited a few days to quit—they might make her leave the base immediately. But it would take a few days to out-process, and Major Haverfeld would probably support her staying a few more days as they analyzed the successes and failures of Operation Zagreus.

She headed to Haverfeld's office to tell him of her decision, when rising voices in the main operations room caught her attention. She turned in that direction and entered the room to find the technical team shouting across each other, voices high-pitched with alarm.

"I *am* trying to stop it!"

"Why is it doing that?"

"Who's controlling it? Get me the pilot on the radio."

"Shit! They've been armed!"

"What the ever-loving hell?"

"We need the Pentagon on the phone. Now!"

Major Haverfeld came running into the room, along with the general who was the overall commander of Special Operations Command at Camp Citron.

"Disarm the drone, Lieutenant!" General Sikes shouted.

"I'm trying, sir. I don't know what's happening."

"What's going on?" Freya asked.

A technician answered her. "One of the drones just powered up by itself and lifted off. It was loaded with Hellfires—and the missiles just armed. We don't know who's controlling it."

"That's...impossible."

"Yeah."

There were so many fail-safes in the system. There was no way to hijack a drone. Not without help on the inside. Someone would have to upload code into the system in multiple places.

The person would have to have access to the Pentagon, the drone operations center in New Mexico, and the computer system here at Camp Citron. A bug like that, it would be detected.

All at once, she realized there was a man—a traitor, no less—who'd been in Virginia and

Camp Citron within the last few weeks. He might've made a trip to New Mexico too. And he would have been permitted into the rooms that contained the computer systems that controlled the drones. He'd been high up in the Special Activities Division of the CIA, and part of his job was using the intel gathered by drones to inform SAD missions.

Seth Olsen. Her mentor, her father figure. His betrayal cut deep on a personal level. He'd been killed in DR Congo less than a week ago, and the extent of his treason against the US had yet to be known.

Her cell phone buzzed. She glanced at the screen. Unknown number. She tucked the phone back in her pocket. Whoever it was could leave a message. A hijacked armed drone was more urgent than any phone call, and if Seth was behind this, she might be able to help.

"We need to talk to the director of the Directorate of Operations at Langley. Find out if Seth Olsen was in New Mexico at any time before he came to Djibouti."

"Shit," Major Haverfeld said. "You think this was Olsen?"

"At this point, I think Seth was capable of anything. He was in so deep with Russia, loading software to hijack a drone is entirely possible."

Oh Seth, what else did Gorev have on you that you could betray your country so completely?

"If we can find the code he loaded, could we shut it down?" General Sikes asked.

She shrugged. That was beyond her pay

grade, but there were men in this room with that technical knowledge.

One of them chimed in. "Sure, but it would take time, which we don't have. What we need is access to whichever computer is operating the drone."

"Why not just shoot it down with another drone?" someone asked.

"None of the other drones are responding to our commands. We're locked out. And the one that's in the air is hovering above our command center. If it drops its payload, we're all dead."

Oh Seth, I hope you're rotting in the ninth circle of hell.

"How long can the drone remain airborne?"

"Seventeen hours."

"Could this be a hostage situation? With us as the hostages?"

"Maybe."

Her phone buzzed again. This time, it was a text message. She pulled it from her pocket, and her stomach dropped when she read the message. *Help. SFC CE and I trapped at al-Farooq home. CE is prisoner. I escaped to find phone. AF is planning something. Big. Gorev working with him. Do NOT contact embassy. SW is traitor.*

The text was signed with Kaylea's code, one she used only in communications with Freya.

Freya's hands shook as she replied. *Hijacking a drone big?*

Kaylea: *WTF*
Freya: *Yes. It's armed.*
Kaylea: *OMG*

Freya glanced up from her phone. The room had filled with all the top brass at Camp Citron. "I think I know who's behind this," she announced. She held up her phone. "Kaylea Halpert and Sergeant Espinosa are at Sheikh Rashid al-Farooq's estate—I don't have details, but it sounds like they were both taken there. Espi is a prisoner. Halpert escaped and found a phone. She says al-Farooq is planning something big."

Everyone started talking at once. Freya ignored them and texted another message. *Can you get to a computer?*

Kaylea: *Yes. I'm already uploading the contents of the hard disk to the cloud.*

Freya sent a silent prayer of thanks to the brilliant minds at the CIA who'd invented that device.

Freya: *URL?*

Kaylea sent the long string of digits that was the web address for the cloud storage system, which was, by necessity, not connected to the CIA networks, followed by the password to access the storage. She sent a second text with the URL for a tracking device they'd planted on a boat bound for Yemen with weapons to arm Houthis.

It appeared Kaylea and Carlos had had a busy morning.

Freya shouted out the numbers to the computer techs, and within seconds, they were in. If the computer Kaylea was using was networked with the one being used to hijack the drone, they could get in and hijack it back. And they'd have the evidence they needed to show al-Farooq was behind this attack.

Freya: *We're in.*
Kaylea: *Good*

A moment later, she texted again.

Kaylea: *Hel*

Freya stared at the phone. Was that help? Had she been found?

What could Freya do? Nothing. Nothing at all if Kaylea had been discovered. All she could do was stare at the phone and wait for another message. Minutes ticked by, but no message came.

13

Carlos had no idea how long he'd been unconscious. Instinct said it had only been minutes, but it could have been much longer. His head hurt like a bitch. He could barely see through one swollen eye, and his chest hurt where the tight straps squeezed, but otherwise, he was okay.

Most importantly, he was alone in the cavernous, unfinished portion of the house. He set to work sawing the plastic zip tie against the sharp edge of the cuff link. There was an easier way to break free from zip ties, but bound to the stud as he was, that method wasn't available to him. Thanks to his sharpened cuff links, however, the plastic snapped apart, and he managed to raise an arm to use the link edge to saw at the nylon straps that bound him to the studs.

It was slow going and the flexing of his biceps even the small amount to raise his arm made the straps even tighter. He dropped his hand down and probed the lining of his jacket for the thin blade he'd tucked in along the bottom seam. He managed to work it free by using the edge to cut a hole in the cloth. The blade was small and thin, but easier to use than the cuff link. The strap split and fell to the floor. He took a deep breath and rubbed his wrists.

Now, to find Kaylea and get out of this hellhole.

But before he did that, there was one thing he needed. He climbed up the studs and plucked the detonator from the C-4 molded onto the post, then peeled the plastic explosive from the surface. The military could run tests on the composition to determine where it came from. The US military's formula differed from other countries', and it might even have a taggant.

He tucked the explosive in his pocket and ran toward the completed part of the house. He could only hope Kaylea hadn't been captured while he'd been knocked out.

K aylea tucked the charging phone behind the computer and ducked into the closet again. After Gorev and al-Farooq left the room next door, she'd crammed the unconscious man into the closet, so now it was cramped with him taking up most of the floor space.

She held her breath. A man in the hall spoke, shouting it was time to evacuate the palace. In the office, the door thumped against the wall as it slammed open. In Arabic the man said, "The children are here, enjoying the feast. We need to go—" He cursed, probably at seeing the room was empty. A moment later, he jerked open the closet door.

Kaylea struck with the heel of her palm, hitting the man in the mouth and nose, snapping his head back.

Caught off guard, he fell back. She struck again with the blade, slicing open his cheek.

He recovered faster the second time, caught her wrist, and twisted her around. She dropped the blade before he could force her to hold it to her own neck. Instead, he caught her in a chokehold, pulling her back to his chest, he squeezed her neck in the crook of his arm.

She struggled, but was no match for his size and strength. She scratched his arm with jagged nails that had broken as she climbed through the ducts. She needed air.

Panic pushed at her as she tried to loosen his hold. She couldn't hear anything but her pounding heart.

All at once, his hold loosened. She gasped for air as she lurched away from him. She turned to see Carlos catch the man by the head. With a swift sharp twist, the man's neck snapped. Carlos shoved him aside and grabbed her.

His face had taken a beating, but he was alive, and she felt a rush of relief and joy even as she gasped to draw in a breath.

"We gotta go, babe. I think this place is gonna blow, sooner rather than later."

She nodded. "I think the drone is going to bomb us."

"Drone?"

"He hijacked a drone. I think—I think children are here—being fed leftovers from the party. He plans to kill them and blame the US. Say we lost control of a drone and destroyed his house, killing children in the process."

Drones had crashed in Djibouti before. The government had required the US military to build a new airfield for the drones in a more remote area, far away from the civilian population. But a "mistake" of this magnitude was likely to get the US military kicked out of Djibouti altogether.

Especially if it were added to a false flag operation that involved an American Special Forces soldier. She realized now al-Farooq hadn't wanted to send Carlos to Yemen to be a Houthi prisoner, paraded in front of cameras. No. He would have been captured by soldiers fighting *for* the ousted president and accused of aiding the Houthis.

"The house is rigged to blow," Carlos said. "Anything the Hellfires miss will be taken down with C-4."

"We need to get the children out of here."

They were unarmed, and who knew how many guards remained in the front room where the food was, but odds were the only people left inside the palace didn't know the building was about to be bombed.

She followed Carlos, running down the hall

to the front of the house. Up ahead, she heard the high-pitched voices of excited children.

What sort of monsters lured starving children with food so they could murder them? These children were Somali refugees. They'd already suffered so much in their young lives. And al-Farooq and Gorev would use their lives as fodder in an undeclared war.

They burst into the room, catching the surprised stares of the children—dozens of them— and she realized how insane they must look, with her torn and bloody dress and Carlos's battered face.

The only adults in the room were two members of al-Farooq's service staff, locals hired to cook and clean. They likely didn't know the plan. More victims.

The staff—a woman and a man—looked at her and Carlos in shock and surprise.

In Arabic, Carlos shouted, "A drone is coming! This house is going to be bombed! Run!"

The children looked at him in confusion and disbelief. After a pause, they resumed eating the treats from the large round table.

Kaylea repeated Carlos's words in French and again in Arabic. She ran to a small girl and plucked her from the floor. "We need to run! Hurry!" The girl struggled in her arms. "Please, baby!" she said. "I don't want you to die."

How were they going to convince these kids to leave the largest feast they'd likely ever seen? She set down the girl and ran to the table. "Take a plate of food with you. Take everything. But run!"

She grabbed a platter of meats and cheeses. Carlos grabbed another tray loaded with bread and fruit.

She looked frantically for a bag or something to put the food in and caught the gaze of one of the servants. The woman cocked her head. "Is this true?" she asked softly in French.

"Yes. We must leave now. Or we will all die." She glanced toward the children. "This is why al-Farooq invited them here."

The woman clapped her hands. "Come, children! Grab a plate and run. If nothing happens, we will come back for the rest of the food."

The children were leery, but one child—an older boy—took a plate and turned for the door. The others began to follow, one by one, until the children realized the best food would all be taken if they didn't hurry. Then it was a melee as they each grabbed their platter of choice.

It took several minutes to get all the children out the door. Kaylea paused before following, listening for children who might have wandered off. No sounds came from the back of the house.

Carlos took her hand. "Let's go."

Together they ran, following the children. As they stepped outside into the late-morning sun, Kaylea heard the whirr of a drone in the distance.

She swallowed the fear that threatened to paralyze her and ran to grab a child who couldn't be more than six. The poor girl was emaciated and couldn't run. She held the girl to her chest and carried her. She grabbed another child, a young boy, but two was all she could carry as she ran to get beyond what was sure to be the blast zone.

Carlos grabbed two children, as did the two adult servants. Some of the older children dropped their food platters and picked up the younger ones.

Kaylea carried seventy pounds of children up the sloping driveway, past the circular fountain to the arched entrance. She ran as she'd never run before, hating that she passed other children as she went.

She'd go back for them.

She reached the top of the drive and crossed under the arched gate. Hope surged in her chest. She crossed the road and dropped the children, then turned back to grab more.

Carlos was already coming back from his second trip as she snatched two more and ran with them back under the arch.

The drone passed overhead. There were still half a dozen children who were within the wall.

Kaylea went back for her third trip and grabbed two children. One of the servants snagged another two, and Carlos, running at bionic speeds, came back and took the last two.

Together, they all ran under the archway as the bombs exploded.

14

The shock wave of the blast knocked Kaylea off her feet. She pitched forward, releasing the children so she wouldn't land on them. She landed hard on the rocky roadway. Heat from the explosion rushed over her. The blast was the loudest sound she'd ever heard times ten.

Her ears ached with intense pressure, and a high-pitched buzz blocked all other sounds. Around her, the children covered their ears as their gazes fixed on the inferno that had been a palace mere seconds ago. They were uphill of al-Farooq's home, looking down on the flaming, collapsed domes. All at once, the back half of the house collapsed. The C-4 explosives Carlos had seen must have detonated.

To Kaylea's ears, the secondary explosions were merely muted thumps.

Wind kicked up all around, and she looked up to see a pair of Blackhawks flying toward an open field to land. The cavalry had arrived.

Carlos crossed the short patch of dry dirt

that separated them and reached out a hand to pull her to her feet. When she stood before him, he wrapped his arms around her and kissed her.

His kiss was deep and fierce, and she kissed him back with equal fervor. They'd survived.

With his hand at the back of her neck, he raised his head and looked intently into her eyes. His mouth moved. The words were faint, but she could just hear them above the buzzing in her ears. "Craziest. First date. Ever."

She laughed even as tears rolled down her cheeks.

He kissed her forehead and wiped her tears with his thumbs. "I love making you laugh."

She smiled and gripped his tattered mess jacket. "I'm crazy about you, Sergeant Espinosa."

He gave her a cocky grin. "I know."

She laughed again and cried again and thought her heart might explode with all the emotions that whirled through her.

Gently, Carlos released her and turned to face the team of men who'd jumped from the Blackhawk and now walked toward them.

Leading the group was Captain Durant, leader of his A-Team. Durant smiled and winked at Kaylea, then his gaze scanned Carlos from head to toe. He shook his head as if exasperated, and then pointed to his watch. She could just make out his words. "You had orders to report for duty by oh seven hundred, Sergeant."

She covered her mouth as she snickered. Half of Carlos's A-Team was snickering too.

"Sorry, sir. I was tied up." He smiled and pulled a baseball-sized lump that looked like putty from his pocket. "But maybe this will make up for it? I got it from al-Farooq's house and have a feeling the chemical formula will match the C-4 that was used to blow up the car in Djibouti City two days ago."

Durant smiled. "Well done, Sergeant." He nodded toward the helicopter. "Let's get you both back to the base. We don't want al-Farooq's men to spot either of you."

Kaylea swept out an arm to indicate the children and servants. "They need medical attention."

Durant nodded. "A bus is on its way to collect the civilians. The rest of the team will guard them until the bus arrives. The FBI is planning to move on al-Farooq, but we need sworn statements from both of you before they can take him into custody."

Inside the Blackhawk, Kaylea leaned against Carlos, and he draped an arm around her. For the last several hours, she'd compartmentalized her fear, and now it rushed in on her how there were dozens of ways in which she or Carlos could have been injured or died. Now her brain traveled all the paths that could have happened, and delayed fear threatened to strangle her.

Carlos must've sensed the tension in her body and guessed at the path of her thoughts because he threaded his fingers through hers and said, "It's all right, sweetheart. We made it. The kids made it."

She nodded and sucked in a deep breath. She would pull herself together. They still had a fake sheikh, a Russian oligarch, and an American traitor to bring to justice.

C arlos and Kaylea were interviewed separately at first. He understood why, but that didn't mean he liked it. Once it was established that their stories matched and the data available corroborated their accounts, they were permitted to enter the main operations room at SOCOM headquarters and were able to flesh out what they knew when their information was combined.

He'd learned about the excitement he'd missed at Camp Citron that morning, when the drone had hovered above the command center for few minutes before it had set off for populated areas including Djibouti City. There'd been no safe opportunity to shoot it down before it took off like a shot for al-Farooq's palace.

During the debriefing, Carlos learned Kaylea had managed to upload much of al-Farooq's computer data to the cloud before the blast.

Brains, beauty, and badass. That was his Kaylea.

After the Hellfires had been dropped, one of SOCOM's computer techs had found the code that was used to hack the drone in al-Farooq's files. Too late to stop the bombing, but the evidence that proved al-Farooq's treachery would help smooth US relations with both Djibouti and Saudi Arabia when the truth came out.

The FBI agents who had investigated the bomb blast two days before had come to Camp Citron for Carlos's and Kaylea's debriefings and promised that no one at the embassy knew of their involvement in the events that had gone down that morning.

The servants who'd helped rescue the kids had been interviewed, and that information was shared as they all worked to piece together the sequence of events. The servants had worked for al-Farooq for only a few weeks. In that time, al-Farooq had actively encouraged them to feed the Somali refugee children, which was an unusual practice as feeding one child usually meant there would be ten more begging the following day. The refugee camp was three miles away, but once the children learned they would get food and water, the distance wasn't a deterrent.

A week before the party, al-Farooq told the servants to tell the children they would be welcome inside the palace for their own feast the morning after the party.

Al-Farooq left for a business meeting as the two servants arrived for their workday. They didn't know most or all of al-Farooq's other employees had also left the premises.

"When did invitations go out for the party?" Freya asked.

"I think Chris said it was about three weeks

ago," Kaylea said. "I was added to the guest list at the last minute."

"That fits with my theory," Freya said. "I believe this plan had been in the works for some time, but the timeline was moved up when the CIA gained Nikolai Drugov's files. Seth Olsen must have realized it was only a matter of time before we came across information about this operation." She shook her head, and Carlos caught a glimpse of sadness in her eyes as she muttered, "An attempt to get the US military ousted from Djibouti. I'm having a hard time reconciling that with the man I knew for so many years." She straightened her shoulders and continued. "My guess is, Seth urged al-Farooq and Gorev to move up the date for the party, even though construction wasn't complete."

"But how did al-Farooq expect the explosion to not be fully investigated by the FBI?" Carlos asked. "The C-4 is sort of a major clue that it wasn't random Hellfires that destroyed the place."

"Right this very minute, al-Farooq is arguing that we shouldn't have access, given that it was a US drone that dropped the bombs, the FBI's 'investigation' would be a sham and our findings would be doctored to exonerate the US of all blame," one of the FBI agents said.

"I overheard al-Farooq tell Gorev that the bombing on Saturday is going to be used as another excuse to keep you out," Kaylea said. "It sounded like they plan to release evidence that a US soldier or other American was behind the bombing, and you—the FBI—used your investigation to cover it up."

"Between your testimony, the files you uploaded, and the C-4 collected by Sergeant Espinosa, we should have enough to fight these claims and take al-Farooq into custody for hijacking a military drone," the other agent said.

"What about Gorev?" Kaylea asked.

"Unless we can find something in the files, he might walk. All we have is your testimony, and given that you didn't see his face, your identification may not be strong enough."

"Which brings us to Stephen Walker," Kaylea said. "I recognized his voice. That's all the evidence we have."

"It might not be enough for a beyond-a-reasonable-doubt verdict. We're talking about charges of treason."

"Stephen knows I was at the house this morning. The only other Americans who know I was there are here or on Carlos's A-Team. If I show up at work this afternoon, it's bound to rattle him. He'll call Gorev to find out what happened, why I'm alive."

"It's risky," one of the agents said. "If he realizes what you know, he might come after you."

"Take me with you," Carlos said. He met her gaze, held it. He couldn't stand the idea of her facing a traitor without him at her back.

Men like Walker, untrained and cornered with everything to lose, were volatile. He knew Kaylea could take care of herself, but in this instance, she didn't have to.

Slowly, Kaylea nodded. "I'd like that." She turned to Major Haverfeld and raised a brow in question.

Carlos's CO gave a sharp nod.

She rose from her seat. "I need to go back to my apartment and shower and change. He'll be even more rattled if I'm in my fully polished persona and claim I didn't show up for work today because I was taking a personal day."

"Espinosa, wear civvies," Haverfeld said. "Officially, you're off duty, visiting Ms. Halpert's office on personal business. You go in looking official, and he'll rabbit."

"Yes, sir."

"Can you record your conversation with him, Ms. Halpert?" the FBI agent said.

"Yes. And I'll plant a bug on him so I can listen if he calls Gorev."

"We don't have a warrant for that, and the CIA isn't allowed to use surveillance on American citizens unless they themselves are CIA."

"I honestly don't care. The guy wanted me to bring Carlos to the party so he could be abducted and sent off to Yemen for some false flag operation. If things had gone according to plan, Carlos would've been killed and his body paraded through the streets. If we catch info on the bug that you wouldn't be able to use in court, we can always corner him with my legal testimony that connects him to Gorev. Anything caught with the listening device might give legal leads to follow."

The agent gave a sharp nod. Carlos figured the guy was just checking a box in raising the legal objection. A reminder that they'd need more than an illegal wiretap to convict this guy.

Haverfeld signed Carlos's orders, including authorization for another vehicle. Papers in hand, he and Kaylea went to his CLU to grab clean clothes. He'd shower and change at her place. As he tossed what he needed into a bag, he glanced down at the tattered blue mess uniform. "Glad I didn't have to pay for this one. These things are expensive."

Kaylea laughed. "You lost an SUV and destroyed a uniform. Can you be trusted with government property?"

He smiled and advanced on her. "Technically, *you* lost the SUV. *I* left it parked by your apartment in the city."

"I suppose that's true." She grinned up at him as he backed her into the door.

"Speaking as a GI, can you be trusted with government property, Ms. Halpert?"

She ran a hand down his chest. "Depends on the person—er, item—in question, Sergeant Espinosa."

His lips hovered above hers. "Me."

"Oh no, I can't be trusted with you at all. I'm liable to rip what's left of that uniform just to get it off you."

"Good." He kissed her. A leisurely, deep kiss he so desperately needed. He cupped her cheek as he raised his head. "I think we should continue this conversation back at your place."

"Agreed."

He stepped back, but she gripped the front of his shirt and pulled him back to her again.

She rose on her toes to kiss him, and her tongue slid between his lips in a sweet, sexy, and tender kiss. She dropped back and whispered, "I'm so thankful we get to have this moment."

"Same."

15

"Shower with me?" Kaylea asked after she'd checked her apartment for bugs.

He smiled, his eyes wrinkling at the corners the way she liked. "It's the right thing to do, really. We both need to shower, and water is precious in Djibouti."

She laughed. She needed this with him, before she put on her makeup and did her hair in preparation for facing a coworker who'd conspired to have Carlos kidnapped.

They both stripped unceremoniously and stepped into the hot spray of the shower. For the first minute, they just held each other, breathing in the steamy air. It was a terrible waste of water, but she figured they'd both earned it today.

Carlos ran a hand down her back, the look on his face almost reverent. "You are the most beautiful woman I've ever known."

She cupped his face, the cuts on her palms embracing his jaw while her fingertips explored the stubble on his cheeks. Her wounds had been cleaned and bandaged by a medic as the FBI agent interviewed her, and Carlos had been examined as well. Now these bandages were wet; she'd have to change them before going to the embassy.

She still had low-level ringing in her ears from the blast, but for the most part, her hearing had returned to normal. They both had cuts and scrapes, and he sported an impressive black eye, but otherwise, they'd come out of the experience in far better shape than they'd had any right to hope for.

"Thank you. Looking at you makes my eyes happy too. And touching your incredible body?" She sighed as she ran her hands down his chest. "Bliss."

They kissed, slowly, softly, as the water poured around them. Eventually, she reached for the bar of soap and began lathering the hair on his chest. Soon she had him coated in thick suds, and her hands played with his slick erection.

He took the soap from her and had his turn washing her. They touched, but the play was light. Not intended to get anyone off, just a connection. A moment to savor.

Scrubbed clean and rinsed, they left the shower, and Carlos toweled her dry, then scooped her up and set her on her bed. He crawled up over her, his naked, wet body pressing her into the mattress.

"Do we have time to make love before we go to the embassy?" he asked.

"Yes. With the drone hijacking, everyone

will be there all night. Stephen isn't going any-where, and the later I arrive, the more sure he'll be that we both died in the explosion, and the more shocked he'll be to see us both."

Her cell phone—still on her nightstand where she'd left it when she ran after Carlos this morning—vibrated, underscoring her words. "That's probably work, wondering where the hell I am. Stephen's been monitoring my phone, so I can't answer it."

"What are you going to tell your boss when we get there?"

"I took a personal day to be with you before you leave on Saturday and forgot to bring my phone with me. Chris'll be angry, but he'll get over it when the truth comes out."

She slid her hand between their bodies and wrapped it around his heavy erection. "I think we should do something with this."

He sucked on her nipples as she stroked him. His hand slid between her legs, then he kissed his way down her body until his mouth reached the juncture of her thighs. He took her to the edge of orgasm with fingers and tongue, then stood, taking one step back from the bed and her splayed, quivering body. "God, you look beautiful like that." He grabbed a condom from the nightstand, then said, "Turn over. I promised to take you from behind."

His voice was deep and raspy. Sexy as hell as he issued orders. She obeyed, getting on hands and knees on the bed, offering herself to him.

He slipped a finger inside her. "I want this

to be mine," he said. "Only mine. Tell me you're mine."

She still didn't know how they were going to make this relationship work, but they both wanted the same thing. She closed her eyes, lost in the feel of his fingers sliding inside her and teasing her clit. "It's yours. I'm yours. And you're mine."

"Yes." He thrust his cock into her in one smooth motion.

She groaned at the intense, wonderful feeling of him filling her. Both the physical sensation and the emotional connection. Hers. He was hers.

He grasped her hips and slid inside her with slow, deep strokes. She dropped down so her head and chest were on the mattress but she remained on her knees, utterly lost in the pleasure of his measured thrusts.

Again, Carlos reverted to Spanish as he came, saying the hottest, dirtiest things about how much he loved fucking her and the things he wanted to do with her next. She loved every sexy, dirty word.

Afterward, he pulled her into his arms. She pressed her cheek to his chest, listening to his slowing heartbeat, wishing this moment could go on and on. "I think I'm falling in love with you," she said.

She met his gaze and loved the heat and warmth in his eyes. In his smile. He traced her nose and lips with a fingertip and said, "I know I'm in love with you."

It had been years since she'd said and received such words—the last time being back when she was still married. She'd forgotten how it felt, the crazy elation that came with falling in love.

"Why didn't you ask me out? That day at the firing range?" she asked.

His brown eyes held such warmth. Joy. She could stare into them for hours. "Aside from being deployed and unable to leave base without signed orders, there was the thing with the bets. You know about it, right?"

"That there's a pool on base over who would be the first to bang me? Yeah. I know about it."

"If I asked you out, I didn't want you to think it was because I was trying to win. I would never be part of a bet like that."

"Freya told me about the time you and Pax got into it with sailors at Barely North, that you tried to put a stop to the betting." That might have been the moment she fell hard for him, knowing he'd stood up for her. "Tomorrow, we can go to Barely North together, and you can claim the pot and buy me dinner with the money."

He laughed. "That would be fitting, but after you kissed me in front of dozens of marines and soldiers at the bomb site, I'm pretty sure the betting disbanded."

"Huh. Guess I should have picked a winner months ago."

He pulled her head toward his and met her halfway, kissing her softly. Then he leaned back and said, "So, why didn't *you* ask *me* out?"

She'd asked herself the same question, because if not for the party, she wouldn't have asked him out. She probably wouldn't ever have seen him again once he returned home. But she'd thought about him a lot in the last few months. Thought and wondered and enjoyed the thrill of their occasional meeting. "I think because I was afraid we'd end up here. Crazy about each other, but with no idea how to make it work once you return stateside."

"We'll find a way." He rolled over so he was above her, holding her, his chest to her side. "I'm in love with you, Kaylea. I'm not going to simply walk away from this. I want it all with you. Marriage. Children. Although it's not a deal breaker for me if you don't want kids. I want *you*. I know it will take time before we know if what this is between us will last, but I want you to know that right now, for me, that's where I believe this is heading."

Her eyes teared at his fearless honesty. He was laying his heart bare for her. She'd given up on the idea of marriage and children when her marriage fell apart. Even though she was no longer in love with him, she hadn't been able to imagine ever falling in love with someone who wasn't her ex-husband, Simon.

And now here she was, in the arms of the best man she'd ever known, as he offered her everything.

"I don't know if I want kids. I did, once upon a time, but I gave that up when I divorced. And now...my job is too dangerous. Your job is dangerous. So all I can say is maybe." At thirty-four, she still had time left on her biological clock.

His smile could have lit the room. "No need to decide that one right away."

The phone on her nightstand buzzed again.

She sighed. "I suppose we'd better get this over with."

"We will continue this conversation."

She smiled. "Yes. We can do it via email if need be. By the way, my middle name is Beatrice."

*

As Kaylea had predicted, her boss, Chris Crawford, was pissed by her extremely late arrival to work in the middle of a major diplomatic crisis, and even angrier that she'd brought Carlos with her. He called her into his office to yell at her in private, while Carlos sat in her office, listening in, thanks to the bug she was wearing.

"Jesus, Kaylea. I was ready to send out a search team for you! Why haven't you been answering your phone?"

"I left it at home by mistake. I'm sorry, but I came in as soon as I heard about the explosion. And you damn well know this is the first personal day I've taken in months. I refuse to feel guilty when"—she lowered her voice to a whisper—"you know I work *two* jobs twenty-four seven."

"And a hijacked drone bombing a residence in Djibouti is exactly the sort of thing you need to be on top of for your other job." His voice was equally quiet, but laced with anger.

Carlos grimaced at exactly how "on top" of the hijacked drone situation she'd been.

"I'm here now, Chris. Bring me up to date on the situation, and I'll draft a statement for you and Stephen to review."

"First, you need to send the soldier home. This is definitely not take-your-new-boyfriend-to-work day."

Carlos imagined Kaylea rolling her eyes.

"He's here with me because he was my ride. We went to visit the Linus site this morning and do a little exploring. It wasn't until we got back to the city that we heard about the drone attack on the radio and he drove me straight here. I think he'll be of help, though. He's a combat engineer. He knows explosions. From the little we've heard, it sounds like there were secondary explosions. He has theories on that."

She was stretching for a reason to keep him in the office, but he liked the attempt. It didn't matter what Crawford said; he wasn't leaving Kaylea until Walker was in custody.

Again, she lowered her voice. "Frankly, Chris, I feel better having a Green Beret here with us. I'm surprised you haven't asked Camp Citron to surround the embassy. We all have watched video of what happened in Iran. We've all studied Benghazi."

Crawford went silent. Finally, he said, "If we have soldiers circle the embassy, it will make a statement, as if we have something to hide. To fear. Camp Citron said the drone was hijacked, that it didn't fly out of control, and they didn't deliberately bomb al-Farooq's palace and then crash the drone into what was left. I believe SO-COM. I believe the pilots. I believe the Pentagon. I will not send a signal to the citizens of Djibouti City that we're guilty by surrounding the embassy with troops.

"But your point is noted and the soldier can stay." The man sighed audibly. "You can imagine how the entire diplomatic community is freaking out. They were all at that palace last night. Every one of them is imagining a scenario in which the drone bombed the palace twelve hours earlier. They're all feeling like they dodged a Hellfire missile."

While Carlos could relate to that idea—in fact, he was certain that was why al-Farooq timed the hijacking to follow the party, so diplomats from every country would feel threatened, as if it were a "but for the grace of God" moment that they were still breathing. He also wanted the political players to see his grand home, to give them a scale for the disaster, before it was gone. So every single country would push for the US to be kicked out of the country.

And, if they couldn't prove what al-Farooq had done, it might still work.

"I know how they feel," Kaylea said. "How you must feel. I was there last night too. I feel the same way."

Except he, Kaylea, two dozen kids, and two servants had *really* dodged a Hellfire missile. He figured Kaylea would enjoy the moment when she got to share that tidbit with Crawford.

"Bring me up to speed, and I'll draft a press release in Arabic and French."

A phone rang. "I need to take this. Find Stephen. He'll give you the rundown. I'll find you when I'm off the phone."

A moment later, Kaylea returned to her office. She again looked like a fashion model. Her dark corkscrew curls were pulled back from her face, this time with a comb headband with tiny beads that caught the light. Her makeup was applied to perfection, and she wore a crisp blouse and jacket, slim designer skirt, and her heroic black boots, which she'd restocked with supplies from her apartment. She'd donned thin, dark, carpal-tunnel wrist braces to cover the cuts across her palms from the air vent. Her other cuts and bruises were hidden by her clothes.

One would never know at a glance what she'd been through that morning. Unlike him. He had a healthy bruise around his eye. The lump on his temple and swelling around his eye had been treated with cold compresses while at Camp Citron. Both were less noticeable than the purple bruises. Kaylea had applied makeup to soften the colors, but there was no hiding it.

"My boss wants me to find our public diplomacy officer for a full debriefing. Would you like to join me?"

He smiled. They would maintain their roles every moment they were inside this building. "Yes. Thank you." He was more than eager to witness Stephen Walker's reaction upon seeing them.

16

Kaylea raised her hand to knock on Stephen's office door, but changed her mind. She wanted to see his face when he discovered she was still alive, and didn't even want to give him the warning of a knock. She pushed open the door and stepped into his office. Carlos followed her into the room. Stephen sat behind his desk, his chair turned to the side as he spoke into a landline phone.

"Sorry to barge in—"

He turned in his chair lightning fast, his body rigid with surprise.

"—Chris says you need to bring me up to date on the situation with the drone."

The phone fell from his hand when he saw Carlos. Then he seemed to recover. He jolted and hung up the phone without a word to the person on the other end. "Kaylea. We've been so worried. When we couldn't get ahold of you today, I didn't know what to think."

She cocked her head. "Why would you think

anything?" She dropped into the visitor's chair in front of his desk.

His gaze returned to Carlos, who remained standing behind her. Stephen went mute for a moment. Finally, he cleared his throat. "I don't —I don't know. We're all feeling so *off*. I mean, Christ. We were all at that house last night. Even you." He nodded to Carlos with his chin. "It's just...scary."

Kaylea said nothing and just stared at him. Stephen didn't like silence. It made him uncomfortable.

"What happened to your eye?" he asked Carlos when the silence went on too long.

"Ran into the butt end of a rifle."

Sweat dotted Stephen's forehead. Kaylea guessed he'd been close to losing his shit all day. Seeing two people back from the dead had to freak him out.

"Kidding," Carlos said. "Baseball injury. Don't doubt Kaylea when she tells you she can throw a mean fastball."

Stephen shook his head as though trying to clear it. "You were...playing baseball? In Djibouti?"

Carlos shrugged. "There's not a lot to do on a day off. I'm tired of shooting at the firing range."

Stephen's phone rang. "I, uh—I need to take this."

"Fine. Join me in my office when you're done so you can bring me up to speed." She pushed up on the arms of the chair and rose to her feet. She hadn't been able to plant a bug on

Stephen's body, but she'd tagged the chair. Hopefully, he'd make his calls from his office.

Back in her office, she locked the door, and she and Carlos both put their earpieces in their ears. Stephen quickly dispensed with his caller and hung up. A moment later, it sounded like he was placing another call.

Thank goodness for stupid criminals. Or at least for the fact that Stephen had probably already swept his office for bugs and didn't know Kaylea was CIA, or he'd have checked everything she'd touched before he made this call.

She could only hear Stephen's side of the conversation, but she could easily imagine Gorev on the other end.

"What the fuck?" Stephen's words were angry whispers. "Kaylea is here. With the fucking soldier."

Short pause.

"It's possible, dammit. I just saw her! She's alive. So is he. Unless they both have twin siblings."

Longer pause.

"I can't possibly—"

Short pause.

"No! That will get me killed."

Long pause.

"You're the one who fucked up. Why should I fix it?"

Longer pause.

"This was supposed to be my last job—"

Short pause.

"I've done everything you asked. I don't

even care anymore." Now he sounded like he might be sobbing.

Short pause.

"I can't do that. She's got a fucking Green Beret with her. You think I'd survive? To protect you? I can't live like this anymore. I can't do this. It never ends. But I want you to know one thing, Gorev, I'm taking al-Farooq down with me. I've got recordings. Photos."

A crash sounded like he'd tossed the phone at the wall.

Kaylea held Carlos's shocked gaze. "What do you think that means?"

"He's not going to rabbit. He's going to blow his head off."

They both jumped from their seats and ran down the hall for Stephen's office. Carlos ran ahead, his service pistol in his hand. He reached the door when she heard the loud crack of a gunshot.

Carlos pressed back against the wall before pushing open the door. He entered the room gun drawn, pointed at chest level.

He lowered the weapon and took a step back. "He's dead."

EPILOGUE

Kentucky
One month later

"Freya, Morgan, Brie, and Amira are all heading to a bar for girls' night out tonight," Cal said. "Pax, Bastian, Rip, and I are going to surprise them since we've finished with the training early. Want to join us?"

Carlos shook his head. "No thanks, man. The last thing I want to see is you guys with your girlfriends when Kaylea is on the other side of the world. I'm going to head home and sext her."

"TMI, my friend. But if you change your mind, join us. Freya wants to hear details about what was on the USB drives that were in Walker's safe."

He laughed. "As if I know."

"Ha! I knew there were USB drives in the safe. Thanks for confirming."

Carlos shook his head. He'd just fallen for the oldest, lamest trick in the book.

He headed into the shower; he had a few nights' worth of grime to wash from his skin before he headed to his apartment. The team had just finished a multiday wilderness training a day early, and he was looking forward to sleeping in his own bed tonight, even though he'd be alone. At least he could email Kaylea, and if she was awake, they might even be able to FaceTime, but with Djibouti being eight hours ahead, that was unlikely.

With thoughts of FaceTiming with Kaylea in mind, he took his time shaving, remembering how she'd stroked his smooth skin the first time they made love.

After Walker's suicide, the dominos had fallen swiftly. As Cal had guessed, the guy had left behind a crap ton of evidence he'd gathered on his blackmailer in a safe in his office. He'd scrawled the safe combination on a piece of paper before he shot his brains out. Carlos wasn't privy to the details, but he gathered there was more than enough to connect the dots and prove that, with the exception of Seth Olsen's and Stephen Walker's participation, the drone attack on al-Farooq's palace had not been an American operation, accidental or otherwise. The American military base in Djibouti remained safe, and al-Farooq had been taken into custody.

Saudi Arabia was demanding him back. Not to free him, but to execute him. He'd been conspiring with Houthis against the Saudis in addition to the Russians.

Gorev remained at large and had likely returned to Russia to lie low for a while.

Clean-shaven and dressed in civvies for the first time in days, Carlos said goodbye to his teammates in the locker room and headed to his SUV.

He was envious of the guys who would get to see their partners that night, but he wasn't complaining about his situation. Kaylea was giving the long-distance thing a chance, and that was all he could ask for right now. He'd take every moment he could get with her, even if it was just a one-word text.

His phone chimed as he settled in the driver's seat. Speak of the angel. His Beatrice who'd helped guide him through the circles of hell.

Kaylea: *Hey. I'm getting ready to go to bed but can force myself to stay awake a bit longer if you'll be home soon and want to FaceTime.*

Carlos: *I'm on my way home now. We finished our training a day early.*

Kaylea: *Oh! I thought you'd finished yesterday. Got my dates confused. Damn time zones. Glad you're back.*

Carlos: *Be home in ten.*

Kaylea: *Can't wait to see you. I love you.*

He stared at the words. She'd said them to him before he left Djibouti, and he still got a rush every time he saw them. Instead of responding, he put the SUV in gear and might've broken a few speed limits in his hurry to get home. Which was funny considering she wasn't there. But still. They'd get to talk and plan the leave she was taking next month so she could go to Bastian and Brie's wedding with him.

He arrived at his apartment and ran up the stairs, taking them two at a time. It was after oh two hundred in Djibouti. He didn't want to keep her up too late, because she had two rather intense jobs and needed to be alert.

He unlocked his apartment and stepped inside, then came to an abrupt halt at the vision on his couch. Kaylea, wearing the silk robe she'd worn that first night and the world's sexiest black knee-high boots.

She grinned. "Surprise!"

"How—how did you get in?"

"Lock picking is easy if you've been trained. Which I have. Also, you need a better dead bolt." She rose from the couch.

He crossed the room and scooped her into his arms. "In the Army, we just blow the locks. Doesn't matter what kind of dead bolt you have."

Her arms circled his neck as she laughed.

He breathed her in. Kaylea. She was here. He kissed her neck and worked his way up to her mouth. She kissed him slowly, languidly. As if they had all the time in the world. And for the first time, maybe they did.

He raised his head and said, "Well hello, Kaylea."

She laughed again. "Welcome home, Carlos." She stroked his cheek. "I do love a fresh shave."

"How long are you here for?"

She bit her lip. "I should have told you first, but I wanted to surprise you, and when I heard you were doing the training, it was sort of perfect how my flights lined up. That you wouldn't notice I was offline for an extended period. Can't believe I screwed up and miscalculated the end of the training, but then, I'm not entirely sure what day it is anymore."

She seemed nervous. Why would she be nervous? He was ecstatic she was here.

"I love the surprise. I just can't believe you're here. How long?"

She smiled brightly. "Six months? I think. Give or take a few weeks here and there when I'll have to be in DC for debriefings and hearings."

He thought his heart would explode. "Seriously? Six months." He spun her around. "That's fantastic."

"Oh good. I sort of freaked myself out on the flight. I had way too much time to think and got scared this was too much without warning. That I should have discussed this with you."

"Honey, the only thing you could have said that would make me happier is if you'd said forever." He sat down on the couch, holding her on his lap. "So what's the deal?"

"The investigation into the drone hijacking has moved stateside. There are going to be a lot of debriefings and probably several hearings with the Senate Select Committee on Intelligence—you'll probably be pulled into those too, frankly. The CIA wanted me out of the field for the duration anyway, so I'd be available, and flights to and from Djibouti would get old if they're happening once a month. I asked the State Department if I could take a leave of absence until the investigation is complete, they agreed, as long as I return stateside for the duration. So here I am. Honestly, it could be even longer than six months, I don't really know. I could still be here when you're deployed again."

She slid her fingers in his hair. "So, here I am, asking you if I can move in with you for an unspecified period of time, but instead of asking, I broke into your home and already put all my bags in your bedroom. And they're really heavy, so I hope you say yes."

His body shook with laughter. "Yes. Absolutely. I'm thrilled."

Her face lit up. "I promise I'll be a great roommate. I'm a terrible cook, but I'm great at doing dishes, and I—"

He kissed her, cutting off her speech. His tongue slid against hers, and he felt like he was home. When he ended the kiss, she was panting and gripping his hair like she never wanted to let go. "You had me at 'surprise,'" he said.

She traced his mouth with her thumb. "And you had me at, 'Well hello, Kaylea.'"

ACKNOWLEDGMENTS

Thank you to the ladies at Indie Intensive who helped my hone my goals for this year and for sharing their collective wisdom.

This novella wouldn't have been possible without plotting help from Gwen Hayes. You're right, you're right. I know you're right.

Thank you Gwen Hernandez for more plotting wisdom and to Gwen (Hernandez, again), Toni Anderson and Jenn Stark for beta reading.

To my readers, as always, thank you for your enthusiasm and support and allowing my characters to enter your world.

Thank you to my children for being who they are, and also for the graphic arts skills they bring to my promotions, and to my daughter for having the patience to teach me Photoshop.

As always, thank you to my husband for sharing this adventure and all the love and support. I love you.

ABOUT THE AUTHOR

USA Today bestselling author Rachel Grant worked for over a decade as a professional archaeologist and mines her experiences for storylines and settings, which are as diverse as excavating a cemetery underneath an historic art museum in San Francisco, survey and excavation of many prehistoric Native American sites in the Pacific Northwest, researching an historic concrete house in Virginia, and mapping a seventeenth century Spanish and Dutch fort on the island of Sint Maarten in the Netherlands Antilles.

She lives in the Pacific Northwest with her husband and children.

For more information:
www.Rachel-Grant.net
contact@rachel-grant.net

Made in United States
Orlando, FL
23 June 2022